MILES LEDOUX

JOHNSON'S WELDER

Winter in Veil, Book 3

First published by ABCs 2025

Copyright © 2025 by Miles Ledoux

First edition

ISBN: 978-1-882508-83-9

Cover art by Rachel Kelli
Editing by Julie Mianecki

This book was professionally typeset on Reedsy.
Find out more at reedsy.com

Preface

Put some pepper on his nose
And you'll make him sneeze-l
Catch him fast before he snaps
Pop! goes the weasel

I

Deputy Benno had been part of Veil's sheriff's department for just over a year. A whole year since this town became his home. A whole year since the most important person in his life had informed him that that life was now over, and he was forced to build a new one on his own, from scratch. A year of jibes and teasing from the other deputies about being the rookie—not that he minded. He'd proven himself a competent law officer, and at this point the "rookie" label was a mere technicality, as no one new had joined the department since he had (apart from Deputy Grogan, but as the senior deputy with years of experience under her belt, no way was anyone going to tease *her*). No, his determination to solve the case he was working on had nothing to do with proving his mettle; rather, it was to distract him, following the anniversary of what should have been one of the happiest days of his life, from thinking about what he'd lost one year ago.

At least, that's what he told himself.

He stood in the center of the parking lot and turned on the spot, scanning the area. Apart from the odd discarded vegetable left over from the most recent farmers' market, he saw nothing of value to his investigation. The lot was quite bare—nothing but faded white lines on cracked pavement.

Benno took another look at Rob Mulroy's planner. Yes, this was where the missing man had made an appointment for midnight on the last day anyone had seen him. Had he arranged to meet someone? But why here? If he needed the meeting to be discreet, what was wrong with the village square in the center of town? Or Riverbend Park, or one of the trails? What made this bleak location more appealing?

Benno headed back toward his patrol car, the loose gravel crunching under his shoes. Then he stopped, walked a few more steps, stopped again. If the grocery store were still open for business, this area would be cleaned regularly. Abandoned as it was, the detritus was allowed to accumulate, making every footstep cacophonous. No one standing in the middle of this parking lot at night could be approached unawares by someone on foot.

A chill slid down Benno's spine.

The mystery of Rob Mulroy's disappearance was not an official case, and Benno had been investigating it on his own, but now it was time to go to the sheriff. Mulroy had vanished too abruptly and too completely, and his last act had been to meet someone in a place that could only have been chosen for its natural alarm system. Someone had expected unwelcome company, and now a man was mysteriously gone. This called for the involvement of more than just one deputy.

Benno radioed dispatch and asked for the sheriff's current location. When he was given an answer, he said, "On his way to the *what?*"

* * *

Halloween Spooktacular, read the banner over the front entrance of Veil's community center. Dozens of families milled about within, showing off costumes, eating candy, and playing games at the booths that had been erected. One corner area was dedicated to pumpkin carving; another had been turned into a mini–haunted house.

"Until this year, they called it Halloweenfest," said a paunchy, thirty-something man with longish, sand-colored hair. "They changed the name because this is the first year they're having it in the new community center, which used to be a grocery store. It's been sitting here for years, abandoned, just like the one on the outskirts where they have the farmers' market. They converted the building last spring, but they almost didn't go through with it because a lot of people thought the place was haunted—like, for real. Except no one could agree on *which* ghost was haunting it—some said it was Johnson's Welder, others said it was the manager who died from an asthma attack in the throat medicine aisle." He chuckled at the apparent irony. "Anyway, I hope that answers your... Heh, actually I can't remember what your question was."

His listener, whose question, some minutes ago, had been, "Do you know what time it is?" said, "Yes, that clears it up, thanks," and hurried away.

"Hey," said the man, catching up with her, "I'm giving a ghost tour of Veil in a couple hours. It starts at the square, if you're interested. I'm Chuck Benz."

She shook his proffered hand. "Nice to meet you."

As she made another bid for freedom, he called out, "Hey, what about you? What's your name?"

"Violet."

"Violet what?"

"I don't have a last name."

His confusion silenced him long enough for her to beat a hasty retreat.

Violet found a side exit, beyond which was a wooden bench on a small lawn. She sank down on the bench and expelled her breath in a great puff, briefly forming a small cloud of moisture. It had been over two weeks since she found herself in this tiny Vermont town, with no memory of who she was or how she'd gotten here. So far her attempts—as well as the attempts of the local sheriff's department—to discover her lost identity had been fruitless. Her physical presence was the sole evidence of her existence.

Since the day of her appearance, a kind family had provided her with a place to live and kept her fed and warm, but she still felt scared, vulnerable. Those feelings had lessened for a brief time when she met a young woman named Candy. A romance had developed between them over the course of several days, and within Violet had sparked a sense of belonging. Sadly, due to a sudden tragedy, Candy was no longer in Veil, and Violet felt as if she were the indirect cause.

She leaned back and closed her eyes, though she wasn't tired. She didn't see the sheriff's patrol car pull up to the building, nor did she see that when the sheriff alighted, he was accompanied by the deputy under whose roof she'd been sleeping, Deputy Jen Grogan.

* * *

"Keith," the deputy said, marking one of the rare occasions when she used the sheriff's first name while on the job, "I want to go on record and say I have a bad feeling about this."

"So you mentioned," the sheriff replied as he held the front door open for her. Once inside the community center, he swept the crowd with his gaze.

"I mean, doesn't this feel like some kind of set-up?"

"This is not something I can just let go. It has to be nipped in the bud." Seeing his deputy's worried expression, he added, "If I end up with egg on my face, you can say, 'I told you so.'"

"Yes, sir," Jen said weakly. The two of them meandered through the main room, silently scanning for their quarry.

"Do you think he's in costume?" asked Jen.

"Of course he is. The same one he wears year-round, disguising him as a normal, decent human being."

Jen cracked a smile.

"Keith!"

Jen's smile disappeared as she looked over at a nearby booth. She had nothing against the man who had called out, now waving the sheriff over and giving him a friendly handshake, mayoral candidate Kurt Riner. It was the woman next to him, Amy Chester, to whom she had a deep-seated aversion.

"Good to see you, Kurt," said the sheriff, following up with a token nod to Kurt's fiancée/campaign manager. "Amy."

Amy nodded back. "Sheriff. Magenta."

"Still just Jen," Jen corrected her, knowing it would do no good.

"You want some stickers?" asked Kurt. On the table before him was a carved pumpkin bearing a close likeness of his face, beside which were stacks of stickers displaying the pumpkin, along with the date of the election.

"Maybe later," said the sheriff. "We've got some business to take care of here."

"Oh, please say Pressler's in trouble," Kurt joked, squeezing his eyes shut and crossing his fingers.

"Actually, yes."

"Wait, really?"

"What's he done?" Amy asked with a kind of hunger in her eyes.

The sheriff eyed her for a moment, then said, "Can you tell us where to find him?"

"Well, his booth's over there somewhere," said Kurt, pointing, "but he's been floating around the last half-hour. Last I saw, he was with a couple Cylons. You know, from *Battlestar Gallactica.*"

"Original series or reboot?"

"Original series, I think. They look like robots with visors in their helmets."

"Is Pressler wearing a costume?"

"Look for a wizard with a white beard," said Amy with a touch of disdain.

"I wanted to come dressed as Superman, but she talked me out of it." Kurt nodded at his fiancée.

The sheriff allowed himself a small grin. "For once, Amy and I agree. No one wants to see you in tights."

Kurt chuckled good-naturedly.

"Hi, Mom," said a voice. Jen turned to see her teenage daughter covered in blood.

After the first heart-stopping moment, she recovered herself enough to note Cyanne's cheerful demeanor plus the prom dress and tiara she was wearing. When Jen found her breath, she said, "No more Stephen King stories for you."

"I'll take that as a compliment, thank you," said Cy with a grin. "So what are you doing here?"

"Apart from having a heart attack, I'm looking for… Where's Violet?"

"You're looking for Violet?"

"No, I just—where is she?"

Cy craned her neck to peer about the room. "I…don't know. She was with us a few minutes ago."

* * *

I

Violet was still outside on the bench, trying to work up the will to go back inside. She knew she was missing out on the fun. Why was she afraid to go back?

She knew exactly why. In a sudden, desperate impulse, she shut her eyes tight, furrowed her brow, and concentrated with all her might….

"Violet?"

She jumped slightly. People had been coming and going sporadically through the side door for the last several minutes, but none of them had taken notice of her until now. A young woman wearing a black turtleneck and a headband with black cat ears now approached her. She had a comely, whisker-painted face—a face Violet recognized. An image came to her of this woman holding a feather and a phial of burning incense. "Marcy?"

Marcy smiled. "You remember me," she said, pleased. This was, in truth, no great surprise, as Violet was able to perfectly remember everything she had seen and done since she woke up in this town, but she didn't mention it.

"Are you doing okay?" Marcy asked, coming closer. "Your friends are looking for you."

Violet knew she meant Cyanne Grogan, the teenage girl with whom Violet had developed a quick bond after they'd met, and two of her classmates. She'd left them by the table with the gingerbread haunted houses. "Yeah, I know," she said, feeling guilty for having ditched them without saying anything. "I just… I wasn't feeling well, so I came out here to…sit down," she finished lamely.

"Too much candy?" Marcy asked, sitting next to her.

Violet smiled wryly. "More like not enough Candy," she murmured.

"Pardon?"

"I said I didn't have that much candy."

"Yeah, I always say that, too." Marcy took a deep breath and let it out contentedly. Then, as if she couldn't contain herself, she gushed, "I love Halloween. It's not like other holidays where you celebrate at home, with just your family. You celebrate this with the whole town, and it's like *everyone's* your family, and everywhere is your home."

The sharing was abrupt, though Violet couldn't help but feel that Marcy's enthusiasm was just a little bit infectious. "You must have been happy growing up here in Veil," she said.

Marcy shrugged. "Mostly. I'll miss Veil when I move away to college—once I can *afford* college—but I know I'll come back and live here when I'm done. I'm gonna be a wildlife biologist." She expounded for a minute on the trivia of local fauna. Violet had little interest, but again she found the young woman's vibrant energy somehow charming and uplifting, so her show of attention wasn't completely feigned.

"Anyway, what are your plans for tonight?" Marcy asked.

Violet said that Cy and her friends planned to take her trick-or-treating.

"I recommend the neighborhood by the riverside," said Marcy. "They usually have the best treats and decorations. Oh, and if you like caramel apples, you should stop by the Thurmins' place on Mountain Boulevard."

"Thurmin," repeated Violet. She recognized the name.

"Yeah, Ms. Thurmin's the one who brought the blood-velvet cake tonight. She's over there"—Marcy pointed through the window—"with her adopted daughter, Emma."

Violet sighed. "I might not know my exact age, but I told Cy I'm probably too old to go trick-or-treating."

"Nonsense!" Marcy spoke with such conviction and seriousness that Violet couldn't help but laugh. Marcy went on, "Besides, with the right costume and your height, you'll have no trouble convincing people you're the youngest of the group. You'll get more treats than anyone. I'm only slightly envious," she added parenthetically.

"If I get a lot of treats, I promise to share them with you," said Violet.

"Oh, so you wanna meet up after you're done trick-or-treating?"

This caught Violet off-guard. "What?"

"My buddies and I, we like to hang out outdoors after all the trick-or-treaters are gone, and try to spot ghosts in the dark. Then we go to my place and watch a not-scary scary movie, like one of the *Friday the Thirteenth*s—except the ninth one, that one really is scary. Good beginning, though. What do you say?"

"Um…" Violet thought of telling Marcy she'd be too tired, but she felt bad for having lied once; she didn't want to do it again. "That's really nice of you, Marcy, but I'm really not up to hanging out these days."

"O…kay," said Marcy. She seemed more curious than hurt. Then she said, "Can I ask you something?" and without waiting for a response proceeded, "What were you doing when I first came out here?"

Automatically Violet said, "Nothing."

Marcy tilted her head forward such that if she were wearing glasses, she'd be looking over them.

"Sorry, it's just…I don't know you that well."

"Okay. I understand." Marcy looked away, as if interested in something else. Five seconds passed.

"I was trying to make my memories come back," said Violet.

"I thought if I focused really hard…"

"At the sabbat, it sounded like you'd already tried that. You said you were just going to wait and see if they'd come back on their own."

"But in the meantime, I'm making friends, and…" Violet thought of her first kiss with Candy, how Candy had helped her come to terms with her situation. "And I'm starting to build a life, relationships. What if I build all of that only to have to let it go when my memories come back, or I find out who I was—am?" She thought of the night Candy left Veil, forced to relocate after she discovered an awful truth—thanks to Violet. "I just think it'd be better to get back to my old life before the new one gets too far along, if it's never going to have a chance anyway."

Marcy digested this in silence.

Violet inhaled deeply. Saying it all out loud had helped a little. The noises of the party drifted out to them. "Monster Mash" played on a speaker. Another party-goer came out through the side door and drifted past the two young women, whistling, though it wasn't the same tune.

"I had an idea for a painting once," Marcy said out of the blue. "I could see it so clearly in my head, I knew exactly what colors and materials to use and everything. But I was afraid that when I went to college—whenever I could afford to, and was accepted—I'd be too busy to finish it. I knew it could happen any time; I was afraid to take the risk." She flashed Violet a half-smile. "I think we're all afraid of risk, with or without amnesia."

In her head, Violet conceded that her amnesia hadn't had any part in what caused the end of her and Candy's romance. "What happened with the painting?" she asked.

"If you come over tonight, you can see it. It's almost done."

Gradually Violet nodded with a small smile. "I'll think about it." Then a thought struck her, and she narrowed her eyes. "Did Candy ask you to look in on me, to see how I'm doing?"

Marcy shrugged off-handedly. "She just wanted to know you're okay. She's still adjusting to things, but she didn't, like, forget you right away when she left. I'm sure she'll get in touch with you when she's ready."

Violet felt a rush of affection for Marcy—and for Candy. She missed her.

"Do you have a phone?" asked Marcy.

"No, why?"

"I want to give you my number in case you change your mind. Let me get a piece of paper."

"No, just tell me. I'll remember."

"You sure?"

"Trust me."

II

"**B**enno!"

Jen Grogan was still trying to help Sheriff Dubowski locate Elijah Pressler. She had just spotted Violet coming back inside, and sent her daughter to intercept her, as they would all be heading home for dinner before too long. The next person to catch her attention was a fellow deputy. "Benno, what are you doing here?"

"I've got to talk to the sheriff," Benno said, trying to mask his eagerness but not quite succeeding. "I've got concrete evidence we should be treating Mulroy's disappearance as a possible crime!"

"Wait, wait a minute." Jen pulled him back as he started across the room toward the sheriff. "What do you mean, evidence? What evidence?"

"I think he was—"

"No, not something you think. What can you prove?"

"Well, technically I can't prove anything yet, but—"

"Benno, you know you're supposed to be looking into Matt Foley's disappearance, not Mulroy's. Foley's been reported missing; Mulroy hasn't. If you go to the sheriff with just theories and he finds out you've been investigating the wrong missing man…"

Benno gave her an incredulous look. "You *asked* me to find Mulroy!"

After checking that Cy wasn't within earshot, Jen took a patient breath. "Yes, I did. Cy thinks I ran him out of town, and I let her believe that. The only reason I'd ever tell her I lied to her is if we find hard evidence that Mulroy didn't disappear of his own free will. And even then…"

Benno sighed in exasperation. He cast another glance at the sheriff. "My gut tells me this is serious," he said. "The longer we put off investigating, the colder the trail will get."

"Then follow the trail a little farther until you get to something more solid. Or, at any rate, don't talk to Dubowski until you've got a lead on Matt Foley. You know how cranky he gets when we don't follow procedure."

Benno made a dismissive noise. "The sheriff never gets cranky."

A sudden strangled cry directed their attention across the room toward a wide booth Jen had passed earlier. It housed an activity called the Haunted Waterfall, wherein participants would cast a "fishing line" into a model made with blue paper. When they felt a tug on the line, they would "reel" it in to find a treasure (such as a toy or sticker) taped or tied to the end of the line, provided by the "spirits" haunting the waterfall. Elijah Pressler, visible at last, had evidently been the most recent participant, for his line had come back with a large hairy spider attached, which had somehow gotten tangled in Sheriff Dubowski's hair. "Sheriff, I'm so sorry!" Pressler exclaimed. "I didn't see you there!" The sheriff tugged at the spider, whose rubber body was covered with a light adhesive, probably for decorative purposes. It finally came away with some of his hair still stuck to it.

"Sheriff," said Pressler, who was unable to completely mask his amusement, "please accept my apology. I should've been more careful when I was swinging that—"

"Pressler!" the sheriff rumbled. The ambient chatter faded as the two men became the focus of the crowd. Aware of this, Dubowski exerted iron self-control as he spoke, through his teeth: "I came to tell you that the sheriff's department cannot fulfill your request to place deputies at your home tonight during your party, for the purposes of 'guard duty.'"

"Well, that's all right—"

The sheriff pointed sharply at him, cutting him off, but managed to keep his voice even. "Whether or not you're elected mayor, you cannot treat my department as your own private security." With that, he stomped toward the nearest exit, Pressler hot on his heels, still apologizing profusely.

When Jen and her fellow deputy caught up to them outside, the mayoral candidate was saying, "I swear, I never thought of it that way, Sheriff. I should've known how it would look from your perspective. I just thought, under the circumstances, it might be a good idea—"

"Save it, Pressler," said the sheriff, running a hand through his hair. "You don't have to pretend when you're out of the public eye. Knowing you, you probably deliberately made me track you down here so you could humiliate me. But it's going to take more than a practical joke to take away the public's trust in me."

"Sheriff, for goodness' sake, why would I want to—"

"Because I support your opponent in the race for mayor. And you know the majority of the town will vote for the candidate I endorse. The fact that you've stooped to childish pranks tells me you know you're going to lose."

As the sheriff strode away without looking back, Pressler

called after him in a voice loud enough to be heard by those inside, "Come on, man, why won't you believe me?"

Jen turned to Deputy Benno and gestured with her thumb. "Still wanna talk to him?"

Benno held up a hand. "I'm good."

***

Under the circumstances.

What had Pressler meant? He'd said it might be a good idea to have deputies on guard at his home tonight "under the circumstances." What circumstances? Jen felt uneasy.

"Yeah, Chuck Benz is apparently the oddball of Veil," Cy said as she and Violet cleared the kitchen table. Jen continued to sit at the end, deep in thought. "If you thought Bethany Williams was an expert on obscure historical details, she's nothing compared to Chuck."

"He said he's giving a ghost tour tonight," said Violet.

"A ghost tour? How? His car got impounded yesterday." Cy paused. "How do I know that? God, this town is small." She noticed her mother and did a double take. "You okay, Mom?"

A deep vertical line had formed between Jen's brows. "Cy, I don't want you going to Elijah Pressler's party."

Cy exchanged a bemused glance with Violet. "Okay."

"Just trick-or-treating and then straight back home."

"Well, trick-or-treating and a couple haunted houses. Nee-sha's been telling me about this one near the school; its theme is this old story about something called the Red Bride—"

"Just—not the party," Jen repeated snappishly.

"Yeah, I got that, Mom." An edge crept into Cy's voice as well.

A tense silence followed, eased when Violet said, "I...still don't have a costume."

Cy opened the drawer nearest the back door and handed her

a pair of sunglasses. "Here. Now all you need is a Nerf gun and you can be a Terminator. We have some in the garage—Nerf guns, I mean, not Terminators. Hold on, I'll get one."

"How am I supposed to see in the dark with—" But Cy was already out the back, and Jen had disappeared through the other door, leaving Violet holding the sunglasses. When she tried them on, she discovered one of the arms was loose.

Jen retreated to the den and sat at the desk with her laptop computer. Her intention was to look at the local newspaper's archive and see if anything had been reported recently about Pressler or his home. However, when the screen lit up, an alert displayed, informing Jen of the arrival of a new email message. When Jen saw the name of the sender, all thoughts of Pressler were driven away.

The back door opened and shut. "Got it!" came Cy's voice. "I just need my shawl and we can go." Her footsteps clomped up the stairs.

Thus assured, Jen opened the email and began to read.

She swore under her breath.

"Mmmmeeep." Roswell the cat leapt onto the desk, purring, attempting to nuzzle Jen's cheek. She lifted him off and back down to the floor, whereupon he simply leapt up again. Jen stood, picked him up, carried him to the kitchen, filled his food bowl, hurried back to the den—

And found Violet standing by the desk, her head bent toward the computer screen.

"What are you doing?!" Jen exclaimed. Violet yelped, jumping in fright. Something tumbled from her hand to the floor. Jen advanced on her and demanded, "Are you reading my emails?!"

"What—no! No, I was trying to fix this!" She held up the sunglasses with the limp arm, then stooped and picked up what

16

she'd dropped: a tiny Philips-head screwdriver. Jen noticed the desk lamp had been switched on. "I tried in the bathroom," Violet said in a trembling voice, "but it wasn't bright enough, so I thought—"

Cy's footsteps thundered down the stairs. Jen darted to the computer and clicked away from the email.

Cy entered the den holding a Nerf gun and a shawl to go with her prom dress, and stopped dead. "What's going on?"

Jen and Violet each cast a tense, sidelong glance at the other. "I, I was fixing these sunglasses," Violet stammered. "Your mom startled me."

After a moment, Jen nodded. "That's right."

Cy eyed one, then the other of them. "Okay, so you're both lying to me. That's nice."

"No, Cy, honestly, she just made me jump," Violet insisted.

Cy moved in closer. "If she only came in just now, how did she have time to turn on her computer and open her email account? Seems more like she was here first, and then you—" Her jaw dropped in realization. To her mother she said, "You didn't startle her, she startled *you*."

"No, Cy—"

"You thought she was *me*. You were reading an email you don't want me to see!"

"Cy, I didn't think she was you—"

"What is it?" She moved toward the computer. Jen instinctively moved to block her. "What is it?! Is it something about Dad?!"

"No!"

"Oh my god, it is! I knew there was something you weren't telling me! I asked you, and you said no! You made me feel all guilty for—"

"That's enough!!"

Violet had never heard Jen raise her voice that way before. Cy quieted but still looked livid.

Jen took a deep, long breath. "Cy…you've read the situation wrong. There is no email pertaining to your father's death. I promise you that."

"Then show it to me." Cy's voice broke slightly.

Jen closed her eyes for a moment. "I can't."

A tear ran down Cy's cheek. "Fine," she muttered, wiping it away brusquely. She turned to Violet. "You tell me what it was, then."

Violet blanched. "I—I don't know!"

"You didn't see it?"

"I, I—"

"Cy, don't drag her into this," said Jen. "Now, you don't want to miss trick-or-treating."

Cy looked from her mother to her friend, trembling with fury. She tossed the Nerf toy to the ground. "To hell with both of you," she muttered before stomping out the back. A moment later, they glimpsed her through the window, biking alone toward the village.

Violet turned to Jen. "I'm s-sorry," she gasped. "I didn't know what was—"

"I think it's time you started looking for room and board elsewhere." Stony-faced, Jen took the laptop from the room.

III

obin Hood and Lieutenant Uhura, both sixteen years old, stood waiting in the village square. Groups of trick-or-treaters paraded by on distant sidewalks, eagerly seeking more treat handouts. Amplified ghostly wails and screams echoed in the distance.

Uhura started to shiver and rubbed her arms. "Maybe we should get you a jacket," suggested the green-hooded archer.

The girl in the red uniform shook her head. "I'll be fine once we start moving."

A rumbling noise made them look up to find a golf cart trundling toward them. "Evening!" cried the driver as he stepped out.

"Um…evening," replied Robin Hood.

"Ready for the ghost tour?" The man rubbed his hands together.

The two teenagers glanced at each other. "We're not here for a ghost tour."

"You're not?" The man whipped out his phone and read the screen. "You're not…Stan and Ursula?"

"No, we're Neesha and Em. We're waiting for our friend."

"Oh. Guess I'm a little early, then."

"Mm-hm, guess you are." The two friends simultaneously began inching away from him.

"Well, happy Halloween, then!"

The two returned the salutation half-heartedly.

"And if my customers don't show up, you two are welcome to take the tour! Your friend can ride on the back." He gestured to the golf cart.

"We're good, thanks," said Neesha.

"It's only thirty dollars!"

"Yep, we're good."

"Per person!"

Em and Neesha were fairly running now, but the tour-giver didn't appear interested in following them across the park.

"You should've brought real arrows," Neesha half-joked as they slowed down.

"You should've brought a real phaser," Em returned.

It wasn't long before they spotted the bloody prom queen arriving by bicycle. They started to approach her, then slowed as, in the act of taking off her helmet, she suddenly threw it to the ground. "Whoa," said Neesha. "What's up with her?"

Squinting, Em said, "Oh, she's pissed about something. I bet she had a fight with her mom."

Neesha wrinkled her nose. "I dunno, I think you might be reading into the costume too much."

"Oh yeah, good point."

When she saw them, Cy put on a cheery smile. "Hey guys!" she called, securing her bike and placing her tiara where the helmet had been. "You ready to start?"

"Uh, yeah," said Em, "if you're up for it."

Cy gave them a strange look that was obviously forced. "Why wouldn't I be up for it?"

Her friends exchanged uncertain looks. "No offense," said Neesha, "but, even without the costume, you look like you're ready to telekinetically wipe out the class of nineteen-seventy-…whatever-it-was."

Even under the makeup, they could see Cy's face flush. "Okay, so I'm not in a great mood, but I'm not gonna let that ruin my night, so let's just—" She stopped, peering at her bike and then all around. "Shoot!" She sank to her knees.

"What's wrong?" asked Neesha.

"The bucket! I forgot the bucket! To carry candy in! I made this bucket specifically to go with…" She gestured to her costume, then slapped her hands on the ground. "Damn it!" She rubbed her face, smearing the fake blood.

Neesha and Em sat close to her, forming a triangle. For a minute, no one spoke. "Ghost tour!" they heard from across the park. "Anyone want a ghost tour?"

"You know," said Em, "instead of trick-or-treating, we could just sit here together."

"Yeah," agreed Neesha. "I'd be cool with that."

Cy eyed them both quizzically. "Sounds lame," she muttered.

Neesha shrugged. "I don't think it's lame. Em, do you think it's lame?"

"Nah, totally not lame."

Cy let out a small laugh. More silence followed. When Neesha started shivering again, Cy gave her her shawl. Although that left only her prom dress, Cy's anger seemed to keep her warm.

* * *

One problem with having a perfect memory, Violet had discovered, was that it made it easier to replay events in one's head, whether she wanted to or not. Again and again, she relived the explosive argument that had just occurred. She tried to

21

envision ways she could've avoided it, which only made her feel worse.

What would she do once they kicked her out? How would she live without an identity? Landing a job might be near-impossible. Was she still technically in the custody of the sheriff's department? Would social services still help her?

It took some time to find enough courage to retreat from the worst-case scenario. Perhaps her friendships with Cy and Jen weren't over after all; maybe they just needed some repair. During her time here, she hadn't grown very close with Jen, but Violet admired and respected her for her kindness and bravery. She'd hoped they would develop their friendship into something a little stronger. As for Cy, Violet's awakening in Veil could have been a lot worse had it not been for Cy's selfless companionship and support. Violet knew things hadn't been easy for Cy since her father died, yet the teenager unhesitatingly gave whatever help she could, and didn't expect anything in return (well, until just now, perhaps).

What had changed? Why were the two of them suddenly eager to be rid of her? Had she become too much of a burden? Had she done something to lose their trust? Why did neither of them believe her?

She wished she could talk to Candy again. Not knowing your own identity left the door wide open for self-doubt, and Candy had helped her when it was at its worst. What would she say to Violet now? Probably that her two friends' errant behavior had more to do with themselves than with her. She'd just have to wait for them to cool down. But what was she to do in the meantime?

A knock sounded at the front door. Violet listened for Jen going to answer it, but then remembered that Jen had left the house a few minutes ago, after someone called her on the phone. (Violet was beginning to grow accustomed to this strange phenomenon of recalling things she hadn't consciously registered at the time.)

The knock sounded again. Violet wasn't thrilled by the idea of speaking to anyone at the moment, but it was either that or continue brooding.

She opened the door to find Deputy Benno on the porch. "Hi, Nelly—I mean, Violet," he said.

"Hi. Jen's not here; she just left."

"Well, actually I want to talk to you."

"Me?"

"Yes." Benno peered past Violet and in a quieter voice asked, "Is Cyanne here?"

"N-no, she's trick-or-treating."

"Oh, good. May I come in?"

* * *

Jen pulled over beside the four other patrol cars whose red and blue lights were flashing. Still in her civilian clothes, she clipped her badge over her waistline as she got out of the car.

The sheriff pivoted as she hurried up to him. "Sorry to drag you back on duty."

"No, no," she said. "I needed to get out of the house anyway. What have we got?"

"Neighbors called, reported what they said sounded like a prank gone wrong. Wanted you here for when we check on the resident."

Jen had been so preoccupied, she hadn't paid attention to where she was. Now she saw that the sheriff's directions had brought her to the edge of town. She was standing on the road before a wide expanse of unmown grass, in the center of which was a small, box-like house that could almost be mistaken for a trailer. In the moonlight, she could just make out bits of junk strewn about the yard. A rusty shell of an old vehicle sat before a tiny garage, with twin ghosts of gravel lines under the tires. The nearest house was up the road and across the street. Despite being (barely) within village boundaries, this house felt to Jen as if it were in the middle of nowhere, in spirit as well as in terms of geography. How loud must the noise have been if the neighbors could hear it?

But the detail that arrested her attention was the name on the dented mailbox beside what remained of the driveway. She pointed and said, "Wait, does that say...?"

Dubowski gave her a half-smile. "Why do you think I called you in?"

Jen looked over and saw Deputy Derrick approaching the front door, wading carefully through the detritus scattered over the path. *"Wait!"* Jen hollered. "Wait, stop!"

Derrick looked back in confusion, his fist raised to knock. Behind his head, a long, hollow cylinder smashed through a window from the inside. Instinctively he ducked. He and the other deputies nearing the house doubled back, keeping their heads low.

A shrill voice screeched from inside the house, *"You vampire punks! You try to get into my house again and we'll see if a bullet to the heart works as good as a wooden stake!"*

Jen cupped her hands around her mouth. "Myrna!"

"And if it's werewolves you're supposed to be, we'll see if the bullets really need to be silver!"

"Myrna, it's me! It's—Magenta!"

Dubowski and the deputies gave her surprised glances. They all knew she preferred the shortened version of her given name.

III

The metal cylinder withdrew slightly. "What did you say?"

"It's Magenta Grogan! We're not here to hurt you!"

The sheriff gestured sharply to Derrick to holster his sidearm.

"We know somebody was harassing you!" Jen went on. "Your neighbors heard the commotion and called the sheriff's station!"

"Miss Redpath, this is Sheriff Dubowski!" the sheriff joined in.

"You're the sheriff?"

"That's right! If it's all right with you, we'd like to come inside and you can tell us what happened!" After a few seconds, the cylinder was drawn back into the shadows. The deputies relaxed. The sheriff started toward the front door.

"Hold on! If my neighbor called you, what's Magenta doing here?"

Jen blinked in confusion, then remembered she wasn't in uniform. "I'm a deputy, Myrna! A Veil deputy!"

"A deputy?! You mean you moved back here? When did that happen?!"

"R-recently!"

"*How* recently?"

Jen threw the sheriff a slightly guilty look.

"You've been back for weeks, haven't you! Or *months* even!"

Jen bit her lip. "Maybe!"

The front door opened. Out stepped a fortyish woman with greasy, bedraggled hair, wearing unwashed, tattered clothing. Apart from a limp in her right leg, she kept an upright posture, helped in part by the long pole she used to support herself—not a firearm, as it had appeared, but simply a metal rod. She locked eyes with Jen and with an affronted gesture said, "And you haven't come by to say hello?"

* * *

25

"I don't understand," said Violet. "Cy told me her mother forced Rob out of town, that he went to New Hampshire to stay with his stepbrother."

"The stepbrother, who I interviewed, doesn't know or care where Rob is," said Deputy Benno, helping himself to some candy corn from a bowl in the kitchen, "which is why no one's reported him missing."

"So Jen...lied to her?" Violet asked with a frown.

"Not intentionally. If I'd found him right away, like she expected, she probably *would've* run him out of town. But here we are, over a week later, and no one has a clue where he is. If I were Cy's mom, I wouldn't want to scare her. Would you?"

"I guess not," Violet said uncertainly.

"Now, you're the only person I haven't talked to—besides Cy, of course—who interacted with Mulroy on the last day anyone saw him."

Flashes of memory appeared before Violet: how she frightened Rob Mulroy to stop his assault on Cy, encouraged her to stand up to him in the square, watched as he heckled Elijah Pressler...

"The last time I saw him was at Pressler's rally, same as you," she said. "Cy mentioned he called her later that night, still harassing her."

Benno flipped open a small notepad. "What time was that?"

"I don't know. It couldn't have happened before we arrived here. Maybe after I went to bed..." She trailed off as another memory floated up in her consciousness. She turned her head, as if to regard it. "I think he called her about eight-thirty," she said. "She was in the bathroom a long time with the water running in the sink. When she came out, I got the sense something was bothering her. That must have been it."

Benno stared at her. "That was over two weeks ago. How can you remember exactly what she did, how she looked?"

"Your guess is as good as mine." Violet tried to sound flippant, yet she heard in her voice the bitterness at the irony: she could remember literally everything but her own past.

"I don't suppose you remember anything that might help me find Matt Foley."

"He's missing, too?"

Benno tilted his head half-dismissively. "His cleaning lady—who he was supposed to pay recently—reported him missing, but more likely he decided to take a trip somewhere and didn't bother telling anyone. He's never struck me as the conscientious type."

"Well, I don't think I can help you there. I only met him the one time—well, twice, technically."

"Twice?"

"When I met him at the sabbat, I recognized him from when I bumped into him a couple days earlier. I'd gotten up early and gone for a bike ride. It was, like, six in the morning. I passed him just coming off the footbridge by Riverbank Road."

"I see." Benno jotted it down. "And you're sure it was him? It's pretty dark at 6 a.m."

"I'm sure. It wasn't just his face. I could also recognize his height, the sound of his breathing." At Benno's curious look, she hastened to explain, "It wasn't that I wanted to remember those things specifically; it just happens whether or not I mean it to. When I first woke up, before Cy took me to the hospital, I was so confused. I couldn't tell my memories apart from what was happening in the present moment. After they patched me up, it's like something took over in my brain, some part of me that knows how to differentiate the two. I look at you now, and I can

27

remember perfectly how we met and everything that happened when we were together"—she winced, recalling the impact of a silver SUV with the car she was in—"but I can tell what's past and what's present. I can control it so I'm not remembering *everything* all the time. …Thank goodness."

Benno was staring at her in fascination. "That's incredible," he said. "So, anything you've encountered, you don't even have to make an effort to see it in your head. You actually have to *suppress* your memories so you don't get a…a sensory overload."

Violet's eyes darted toward the door leading to the den. "It's not really suppressing," she said, "but I can choose not to call up certain memories—unless something triggers them."

Benno gazed at her a moment longer, then rose to his feet. "I'd like you to come with me, if it's all right with you."

Violet gave him a sidelong glance. "Come with you where?"

"The last place Rob Mulroy was known to have been."

"Why?"

"Call it…an experiment."

IV

"**A**ll right, get up."

Cy, Em, and Neesha got to their feet and stretched their legs. "You feeling better?" Neesha asked.

"Not really. But I'm not gonna spend Halloween night sitting here feeling miserable. I'm gonna go to a party!"

Neesha eyed her knowingly. "And be miserable there?"

"Exactly!"

"Okay," Em agreed. "Which party?"

Cy turned to face the mountains on the edge of town. Up the slopes, electric lights shone here and there: Veil's wealthier citizens, reminding everyone where they lived. "The one I was told not to go to," she said.

* * *

"Go ahead and confiscate any firearms you come across," Sheriff Dubowski said in a low voice to Deputy Derrick.

Evidently not low enough. "Firearms?!" Myrna called from across the room, which was swarming with random dirty dishes and discarded items of clothing. "Are you crazy? No firearms here. Those things are dangerous. Plus they're too much work—filling out forms, remembering all the rules—which keep changing—and cleaning the damn things all the fricking time. Guns are a goddamn headache. Now, knives—they're much easier to manage. Not to mention cheaper. Most of these, I made myself!" She nodded at the far wall, where dozens of knives were displayed in hand-crafted racks. In fact, out of anything in the small house, the knives seemed the most organized.

"Myrna," said Jen, sitting across from her in what at one point in time, before its burial beneath layers of odds and ends, had been the living room, "You were about to tell me what happened, what scared you."

"What'd you move back here for?" Myrna dodged. "You hate Veil almost as much as I do."

"I don't hate it. At least, not anymore."

"So you missed it?"

"N-no." Jen shifted uncomfortably. "My husband's gone. My family needed a change of scene."

Myrna regarded her for several seconds. "Fine, then, don't tell me. So I was in here, fixing my refrigerator—I fix things for a living, did you know that?"

"No, I didn't."

"No, you didn't, because you haven't spoken to me in fifteen years! So I was fixing that refrigerator and I hear somebody tapping on my window. I look over, and somebody's just ducking away. I shout, 'Who's that?' There's more tapping, but it's on that window now, over there. Same thing, they move away before I can see who it is. I start to think it's just a prank." Glancing at the windows, Jen saw that they were small, dirty, and difficult to see through, but thanks to a yard light outside, she could make out the silhouettes of the deputies combing the property.

"Then I hear another tapping, and it's *that* window." Myrna indicated one near the front door. "I had my porch light off 'cause I didn't wanna attract trick-or-treaters, so I couldn't see him clearly. So I turned it on and…and I saw him."

"You saw who he was?" asked the sheriff.

"Yeah," Myrna said cagily. When she didn't go on, Derrick paused in his search and looked at her.

"Can you tell us?" the sheriff gently prodded her.

"Yeah, I can tell you. But you're not gonna believe me." Myrna avoided eye contact with all of them. "You're gonna say I'm lying or I'm seeing things."

Softly Jen said, "You know I'm not going to say any of that."

Myrna turned her head and their eyes met, and they held each other's stare. Finally Myrna swallowed. "All right. It was the Welder."

"The Welder?" the sheriff repeated. "You don't mean—"

"Yup. Johnson's Welder."

Deputy Derrick scoffed.

"Did you say something, Deputy?" the sheriff asked sharply.

"No, sir."

"I knew it," Myrna grumbled.

"You mean you saw someone wearing a welder's helmet," Jen encouraged her.

"Yeah, and holding a welding torch. Or some kind of flame torch at any rate; I couldn't see clearly. I shouted at him to go away. I told him I had a gun. He started popping up in all the windows, tapping different walls—like he was everywhere at once. I might've freaked out a little bit, started yelling. Probably what the neighbors heard."

The sheriff was frowning. "When we arrived, you were saying something about vampires and werewolves."

"Yeah, well, how do you explain that guy being alive after all this time without him being some immortal creature like that?

31

When you guys showed up, I thought you were more of the same." She hunched herself over, her cheeks reddening.

"It's okay, Myrna," Jen reassured her. "We believe you."

"Hey!" snapped Derrick. "The sheriff didn't say that! Don't put words in his mouth."

The sheriff rounded on him angrily. "Derrick—!" His cell phone rang before he got any further. Derrick quailed under his glare as the sheriff stepped aside to take the call.

"Myrna, I promise we're going to find out who did this," said Jen.

"You think it was some prank? I'm telling you, this guy was *everywhere at once.* I've never given much thought to whether ghosts are real, but this was pretty convincing."

"Maybe it was two people working together, or more."

"Yeah, but why go to all that trouble?"

"People are cruel."

Myrna tilted her head, considering. "Yeah, that's true."

Dubowski stepped back to them, just hanging up his phone. "That was another Veil resident claiming they were tormented by someone in a welder's mask. Deputy Derrick," he went on in an acid tone before anyone could respond, "is there something you want to say to Miss Redpath before we go investigate?"

"S-sir?" Derrick stammered, taken aback.

"I assume the reason you didn't apologize to her was that we had no corroboration of her story. Now we have."

"Yes, sir. Miss Redpath, I'm sorry. …For not believing you." When the sheriff continued to stare at him beadily, he added, "And for…being rude."

The sheriff nodded. "Good enough. Miss Redpath, two of my deputies will remain here to continue searching for evidence. We'll be in touch. Grogan, Derrick, with me."

As they followed him out, Jen asked, "Who was the second target?"

"Oh, nobody important. Just the next mayor of Veil."

* * *

Violet was not at all sure how much help she could be to Benno in his investigation. Even if something did trigger a memory, it would only confirm where Rob Mulroy had been, not show where he was now. Still, since Candy's sabbat, she hadn't had a chance to help anyone, and helping people had so far been the only thing keeping Violet from feeling like a freeloader.

Right away, though, when they arrived at the parking lot, she realized a significant problem: "It rained that night. Any clues that might have gotten left behind have been washed away."

"Yeah, I know," Benno admitted. "But this is the only lead I have, and you're my best shot at turning up *something* to go on."

Violet took a few tentative steps onto the lot. She'd seen it a handful of times; each set of memories vied for her attention like swarms of noisy insects. She waited a few seconds and gradually the noise died down. "So, basically," she said, "you want me to reach back, sift through my memories, and see if any of them relates to Rob Mulroy."

Benno shrugged. "The method's up to you. I'm just going with my gut here."

"I've never actively tried to remember anything before— other than my past," said Violet. "Usually when I remember something, I can't help it."

"Like sitting on a haystack and getting poked by a needle."

"That's…surprisingly apt."

Benno nodded. "Look, if this doesn't turn anything up, it's no big deal. It was just an idea."

But it is a big deal, Violet thought. *As long as Rob's whereabouts are unknown, Cy could still be in danger.*

She closed her eyes and took slow, deep breaths. She didn't yet understand what it was in her mind that kept the memories from flooding forth at every trigger, but, concentrating, she sought it out, picturing it as a translucent cloud dimming what would otherwise be over-bright beams of light. When she felt as if she'd found it, she made the cloud dissipate. As the memories started to shoot their way in, she gasped, trying to flex that mental muscle, adjusting it till the flow was steady, the light less blinding, so that she could wade through the memories at her own pace.

Opening her eyes, she blinked rapidly, wincing, flinching.

"Are you okay?" asked Benno.

"The wheel marks," gasped Violet, nodding at the ground a few meters away. "They're from the trailer with the squash. It was parked closer to the building last I saw it." She squeezed her eyes shut, as if a glaring light were shining in her face. "The booths keep changing positions. All except the one with the apple cider. He always gets here early, parks in his favorite spot under that big tree." She cried out as if in pain.

"Hey, hey! What's wrong?"

"There's so much—I'm seeing all the details at once—and they're all bringing up memories of other little things."

"Anything about Rob Mulroy?"

"I don't think so—I can't tell—" She cried out again, clutching her head.

"Okay, stop!" Benno took Violet gently by the arms. "You can stop now. I don't want you to hurt yourself. It's okay. It was a long shot. Come on, come back to me."

"Back…to you?"

34

"Come on, Violet, you're scaring me."

"No, wait…" Violet closed her eyes, seemed to steady herself. Benno let go of her but stayed close. Eyes still closed, Violet shook her head. "Magnet," she muttered.

"Magnet?"

"I was going about it the wrong way. You don't sift through the whole haystack to find the needle. You use a magnet."

Thinking back to the two times she'd encountered Rob Mulroy, she let the scenes unfold before her, moment by moment, glancing from one to the other in her head. She saw him brush yellow leaves off his jacket. Watched as he strode arrogantly across the square, heckling Elijah Pressler. Looked in the direction he pointed when he revealed the cameramen on the roof.

When she saw him assault Cy, grabbing her, restraining her, she felt something click somewhere, like a jigsaw puzzle piece finding its match. But what did it match? She set that moment beside her memories of the farmers' market. Nothing seemed to relate. It must have clicked with something else; if she hadn't been so enmeshed in her memories of this parking lot, it would've been clear to her right away. Whatever it was, it could wait.

She watched Rob hightail it over the hill, studied the look of horror on his face when Cy mentioned the words, "Skin allergy," saw him tossing a football in the air and spinning it on a post—

Her eyes shot open and her whole body jolted. "Violet?" Benno put a hand to her back as she wavered. "Are you all right?"

Violet blinked. All at once she swung her head around and stared at the far side of the lot. Without a word, she marched off in that direction, Benno following in bewilderment.

At the edge of the pavement stood a row of concrete pillars. Violet had her eyes fixed on one in particular. As she approached, she glanced down, stopped, and picked up a smooth, oval-shaped rock. Her hands were small, but she could almost grasp it one-handed.

"Rob was here that night," she murmured. "Here, at this spot."

"How do you know?"

Violet placed the rock atop the concrete pillar. "The day after I woke up in Veil—the morning after Rob was here, in this parking lot—Cy and I walked through here to get her bike back from Riverbend Park. This rock was here then. I remembered it when I thought of Rob in the park, tossing a football, setting it on top of a post, just like that. It must be a habit of his."

Benno turned on a flashlight and played it over the ground around the pillar. After a minute he stooped and gently sifted through the gravel using his finger. "You're right," he said, rising. "He was here. And I've finally got the physical evidence to prove it." Between his finger and thumb he held a button, almost an inch across.

Violet squinted at it. The button was a light grayish blue. "That's not Rob's button."

"What?"

"The buttons on his shirt were darker. This one..." She closed her eyes, relaxed her control slightly—she was starting to get the hang of it now—and waited for that spark of recognition, if there was any to be had. She resisted the urge to force the connection. If she concentrated on the image of the button, it would happen on its own....

"There was a man," she said, her eyes still closed. "A man at the rally in the square. One of the volunteers gathered by Pressler. The button was on his jacket."

36

"Can you describe him?"

In her head, Violet felt like a disembodied spirit, floating about and spying on this man, examining him. "He was in his sixties. Gray hair. Tall. I mean, actually tall," she added, remembering she was shorter than most adults. "Kind of shabby-looking. His jeans were dirty, fraying at the cuffs. He was wearing old, muddy shoes. And his shirt was—" Her eyes burst open. "There were letters on his shirt! K, V, and another letter after that. I couldn't see—"

"K-V?" Benno had been scribbling the details in his notebook, which he now pocketed. "Interesting. Let's go."

"Where are we going?"

"Downtown."

"Why?"

"The only thing it could stand for is KVLM, our radio station."

V

M usic and dark, menacing laughter reverberated from Pressler's immense house. Cobwebs covered the front door, from which hung a sign with words that dripped blood: *COME ON IN*.

As Cy, Em, and Neesha approached the door, one of them stepped on a hidden pressure pad. A giant spider with glowing red eyes sprang out at them with a shriek, then withdrew back into the bushes.

"I can already tell this was a good idea," said Em giddily.

"You're weird, Em," said Neesha, whose hand was pressed over her heart.

"Why didn't your mom want you to come to this guy's party?" Em asked Cy.

"He's running for mayor against the guy my mom's boss is voting for."

As Cy opened the door, Neesha threw a confused glance at Em. "No, I didn't follow that either," they said.

Pressler's house couldn't have been that much bigger than Cy's, but it felt bigger as soon as she stepped inside. Dozens of people milled about in the front room and on the staircase, and even more on the interior balconies, which reminded Cy of a shopping mall. All the rooms downstairs were decked out in orange and black decorations, with witches' cauldrons filled with sweets on every available surface. There were more adults here than had been at the Spooktacular; what few children there were had gathered in a corner, playing Pin the Head on the Horseman.

"Cyanne!"

Cy was momentarily taken aback before she recognized the man approaching. Pressler had changed costumes from a wizard's robe and beard to a tuxedo, holstered gun, and martini. "Hi, Mr. Pressler," she waved. "Okay if we crash?"

"Of course!" He shook her hand. "And you're not crashing, this party is open to the public! Everyone's welcome!"

"Even Sheriff Dubowski?"

"I invited him specifically!"

"Reverse psychology?"

"Precisely! Who are your friends?"

Cy introduced them: "This is Neesha and this is Em."

Pressler shook their hands. "Is that short for Emily?"

Em flinched slightly but covered it with a smile. "It might be," they said with some forced brightness, "or it might be short for Emmett. *Or* it might be just Em. I haven't quite figured it out yet."

Pressler nodded warmly. "Understood. Please go help yourselves to pumpkin punch." He pointed the way with the martini glass, whose contents, olive and all, didn't spill.

"I like him," Em said as the three of them waded through the crowd.

"Yeah," said Cy, glancing back, "he's actually pretty cool."

* * *

"Johnson's *what?*" said Kurt Riner.

He and the sheriff stood on the porch of his house while the deputies scouted the interior. "Johnson's Welder," said the sheriff. "It's a local superstition."

"I've lived in Veil my whole life. How have I not heard of this?"

"Sheriff?" Deputy Hayden stuck her head out the front door. She was short and stocky, in her late forties, with a natural crease between her brows that made her face seem like it was in a perpetual frown. "First floor is secure. We're checking upstairs."

"I don't think he went upstairs," remarked Kurt. "He just chased us out into the garage. He didn't act like a burglar." He leaned in toward the sheriff as Deputy Hayden headed to the second floor. "Isn't that the deputy who has a crush on you?"

"Kurt, focus," Dubowski said sternly.

"Man, I'm just saying, you could do worse."

"How did the intruder get into your house?"

"Well, that's what I'd like to know. We only leave our door unlocked in the summer, to let in the breeze. Hey, when you say Johnson, do you mean Silas Johnson, the first mayor of Veil? I know he supposedly haunts a few places around town."

"Johnson Thorne, the son of Solomon Thorne, the lumber baron."

"Oh!" All trace of jocularity vanished from Kurt's visage. "Oh, *that* Johnson. Well, that makes more sense. So this 'welder' is…"

"The man who tried to kill him, disguised as a metal worker."

"I see. Didn't know that part."

"When Thorne pulled out a gun to defend himself, he hit the assassin's acetylene tank, which exploded, crippling Thorne for life."

"And the welder was killed in the explosion?"

40

"Most people thought so, but they never found any trace of his body, which gave rise to the legend."

Kurt gave a dry laugh. "Someone's gone to a lot of trouble to give that legend new life. I can think of better ways to celebrate the town's history."

Jen appeared in the doorway with Hayden and Derrick in tow. "The house is clean, sir," she said. "Nothing's disturbed except a few items knocked over downstairs. It looks like he left right after making his appearance."

To Kurt the sheriff said, "We're gonna stick around a while to do a closer inspection. It's possible he left something behind in the commotion, something we could use to trace him."

"I'll stay, too," said Kurt, "see if I can spot anything that's not ours."

"What about Amy?" They glanced toward one of the patrol cars, where Amy sat in the passenger seat, pale, staring straight ahead.

Kurt lowered his voice. "She's a bit shaken up. I think she should check into a motel tonight. I'll join her later."

"Good idea." The sheriff turned to the deputies. "Grogan, take Ms. Chester to the Platte B and B."

He caught her brief hesitation before she answered, "Yes, sir."

The sheriff blew his breath out as he headed inside. He'd shared drinks with Kurt in this house enough times to be familiar with it. He could already see a lamp, a small table, and some hockey paraphernalia knocked over by the intruder's rampage. "At least there's no fire damage," he remarked. "The way this guy's going around, waving a flame torch, he could cause some serious—"

"Flame torch?" Kurt shook his head. "He wasn't holding a flame torch."

"Hm. Well, maybe he dropped it somewhere between Myrna's and here."

"Myrna? You mean Myrna Redpath? That's where he hit first?"

"You know her?"

"Of course I know her. She's my tenant."

"Your tenant?"

"That's right. I own the property she lives on."

* * *

"It's your fault."

Jen, struggling between focusing on the job at hand and trying to think what she could possibly say to her daughter when next she saw her, glanced distractedly at her passenger. "What?"

"A few weeks ago, you called me a bully. You said I harassed you back in school. Well, if I did, it was your fault. You can't blame me for how I treated you." Amy was still staring straight ahead, her eyes barely blinking. Her chest rose and fell rapidly.

Jen glanced at her uneasily. "I think you're in shock. We'll be at the bed and breakfast in a minute, and it won't be long before Kurt joins y—"

"Aren't you going to ask me?"

"Ask you what?"

"Why it was your fault."

At a loss, Jen shrugged. "No, I'm not." *Though I know you're going to tell me anyway.*

To her surprise, the next thing Amy said was, "So you don't hate me anymore? You've forgiven me?"

Jen looked at her askance. From her tone, Amy sounded skeptical, but perhaps just a little bit hopeful. She must be terrified, Jen reflected, for her to even consider asking for forgiveness. "I...don't hate you," was her reply.

Apparently it was the wrong one. "You liar," Amy snarled. "You can't stand me. You think I deserve to die. You think that—man who came into my house should've killed me."

As she slowed for a stoplight, Jen found herself forming a hunch, and she decided to play it. "Amy, what I think or feel has nothing to do with the intruder in your house. For what it's worth, what I really think is that you're scared, and you think having a clear conscience will make you feel safer. And having me right next to you makes that more of a challenge."

"So you *do* hate me!"

"Amy!" Jen was exasperated.

"I knew it. I never bought your crap about having more perspective. That's loser-talk. 'Oh, Amy, my memories of you don't even *compare* to the hell I've been though, so I don't even *notice* you anymore!' You're a liar, just like you were back then."

Jen spotted a stop sign just in the nick of time and braked. "Amy, I don't know what you want me to say, but—"

"I want you to die!"

Her words stunned both of them. For a moment they sat still, the car idling before the stop sign. Jen said quietly, "Well, I can't help you with that."

Amy swallowed audibly. "I'm sorry."

Jen regarded her with wide eyes.

"I…didn't mean to say that."

Didn't mean to say it or didn't mean it? thought Jen, though what she spoke aloud was, "Take some deep breaths. Slow ones. You'll come back to yourself."

Amy obeyed. She seemed to be calming down. Just as Jen was about to proceed past the stop sign, Amy asked, "Is it true? Did something happen after high school? Did you really go through hell?" She did not sound sympathetic, only aloofly curious.

Jen looked away, out the window. Close ahead was a mileage sign listing the distances to the towns along this route. They were close to the edge of Veil. "I don't want to talk about it," she said.

Amy was also looking out the window, but her eyes weren't focused on any object in particular. "What about what you told us in sixth grade? About your high school friend, Violet? About what happened to her? Was that true?"

Jen didn't answer. A tear rolled down her cheek.

"Is that why you moved away? Because no one ever believed you?"

Jen winced. Amy's apparent attempts to be understanding were more torturous than her bullying. Taking her foot slowly off the brake, she said brokenly, "We're almost at the B and B—"

WHAM. Something collided with the car on the passenger side. Amy shrieked. Jen slammed on the brakes and looked over—someone was standing there, outside Amy's window—*someone wearing a metal hood with a thin strip of glass to see through.*

"Oh my god!" Amy screamed. *"It's the Welder, oh my god!!"*

Slamming the car into park, Jen slid fluidly out her door, drew her sidearm, and pointed it over the roof at the hooded assailant. "Freeze!!"

The Cylon threw up its arms. "I'm sorry!" it wailed. "I'm sorry, I didn't see the car there! This thing's really hard to see in, I didn't even know I was in the road—please don't shoot me!!"

Jen had already lowered her weapon, and she hastened to calm down the teenage trick-or-treater.

* * *

"That's him." Violet pointed to the gray-haired man standing at the back and a little off to the side, the only one in the photograph who wasn't smiling.

Rod Piper bent over Violet's shoulder—at six-foot-two, he dwarfed her—and squinted beneath his mane of curly, dark hair. "That's Tuck Fleagle," he said in the deep voice that most everyone in Veil knew from listening to the radio. "He's our sound equipment maintenance man. Or at least he was."

"Was?" Benno repeated.

"He hasn't shown up for work in over two weeks. We've been going crazy trying to find someone to replace him."

"Why wasn't he reported missing?"

"We just assumed he stopped bothering to come in. Lately he's been more interested in drinking here than working; we've found three of his hiding spaces for alcohol." He pointed to the photo of radio station employees celebrating the new year. "The only reason he showed up for that was the free booze. We'd have replaced him before now if there were anyone else qualified who's local."

Benno took another look at the man in the photograph. "Did he leave any personal possessions here before he stopped coming in? Like, in a locker?"

"He had a whole office. You're welcome to have a look."

Before going to investigate, Benno said to Violet, "Are you able to get back home on your own?"

"What?"

"I'd love for you to stick with me, but now that you've helped me pick up the trail—thank you, by the way—I really shouldn't drag you along."

Violet shrugged. "I have nothing else to do. Can't I get dragged along a little longer?"

Benno looked at her askance. "Violet, it's Halloween. Go enjoy yourself. Go hang out with Cy."

Violet looked away with a grimace. She'd been grateful for

the distraction this past hour and hated that Benno was now taking it away. "Cy's—mad at me. For something I didn't do." She felt guilty at the bitterness in her voice. She knew she owed Cy a lot. Did she even have a right to feel bitter?

"Well, then, go tell her," said Benno.

Violet looked at him in confusion. "Tell her what?"

"Tell her you didn't do it, whatever it was. I mean, you still want to be friends with her, don't you?"

"Of course I do."

"Then what's the problem?"

Violet almost laughed. The problem was obvious, wasn't it? Or was she just not comfortable saying it out loud? Her lips tightened as she bit the bullet. "How can I ask Cy and Jen to…to keep me in their home, their lives, if all I am is an extra burden? They're already dealing with a lot. They were bound to be done with me eventually. Shouldn't I just accept it and try to find some way to be useful? I can't keep being a freeloader just because of my circumstances."

Benno was eyeing her with a deadpan expression, chewing his tongue. "Violet," he said, "what you did tonight was extraordinary. I don't know of anyone else on Earth who could've found the connection and led me to this Fleagle guy. You have an amazing gift. I don't think you're *capable* of being a freeloader. What you are capable of, evidently, is self-pity."

Violet sputtered out an incoherent syllable or two.

"Now go find your friend and make up with her." He patted her arm, gave her a friendly smile, and left her staring after him, at a loss for words.

* * *

The sheriff and his deputy strode up to the front door of the house on the corner of School Street and Fairview Lane, where they found two buttons installed. One looked as if it had been built along with the rest of the house; the other looked newer. A laminated sign duct-taped above read: *Please ring both doorbells. Thank you.* Sheriff Dubowski obliged and pushed both buttons. One elicited a familiar *ding-dong.* The other resulted in a rapidly flashing light, seen through the front window.

When no one answered, the sheriff resorted to a more conventional approach: he banged on the door. "Delphine!" he called. "Althea! It's Sheriff Dubowski. Are you all right?" Still no answer. He nodded to Deputy Derrick, who tried the door.

Jen ran up the steps and onto the porch just then. "What've we got?"

"Delphine called the station and reported a prowler," the sheriff told her. "She was cut off mid-sentence—"

"Sheriff!" Derrick darted inside. The others followed.

Collapsed next to an old piano was the elderly Delphine, the phone receiver nearby. Quickly the sheriff knelt and checked her vitals. "She's alive," he reported. "Derrick, get an ambulance here right away. Let's find Althea."

"Sheriff." Jen nodded toward a small table next to the piano. It was covered with a thin quilt that hung to the floor, and though there couldn't be much space beneath it, the toe of an upside-down shoe protruded from behind the quilt.

The sheriff approached the shoe. "It's all right, Althea," he said. "I'm the sheriff and these are my deputies." When the owner of the shoe didn't respond, he reached for the quilt.

"Wait!" Jen pulled his hand back and stepped past him. With the flat of her hand, she thumped three times on the top of the piano. The shoe twitched. The quilt was pushed aside. Seeing them, Althea squirmed frantically, trying to exit her tiny hiding place.

"It's okay," Jen said, helping the septuagenarian to her feet. When her right hand was free again, she signed the letters *O* and *K*.

The sheriff nodded. He'd forgotten Althea was deaf. Jen had banged on the piano three times so that Althea would feel the vibrations—in order to let her know, without frightening her, that they had seen her and were approaching.

Althea signed urgently to Jen, who said, "No, I'm sorry, I don't know sign." She tapped her forehead and pointed to Althea's hands, shaking her head.

Althea directed a pleading look at the sheriff, who said with extra enunciation, hoping she could read lips, "It's all right. The ambulance is on its way." The elderly woman shook her head in desperation.

"You don't know any sign language at all?" asked Derrick.

"No," Jen said helplessly. "That's Benno's thing. All I know is the alphabet." She signed *A, B, C* to Althea with a questioning look.

Immediately Althea began signing one letter at a time. "H," said Jen, "E, S, T, I, L—oh my god. Sheriff, I think she's saying he's still here!"

At that moment, all the lights in the room went out at once. The old woman jumped; Jen caught her and squeezed her hand to try and calm her.

"Everyone get down!" Dubowski shouted, but before Jen could pull her charge to the ground, there was the sound of a door creaking open.

A small, blue flame hissed into life, illuminating, behind it, a metal hood with a transparent visor, reflecting the crackling flame.

VI

F inding the haunted house near the school wasn't difficult (though technically it was more of a haunted garage). The people running it told Violet they hadn't seen anyone in a Carrie costume, but the haunted house was free, so she went ahead and took a tour. She was impressed by how many scares and dioramas were set up in so small a space. More than that, though—it was fun! Stepping into another world, a made-up story—even a frightening one—she let herself set aside her own dramas and enjoyed the ride.

Only afterward, when she was roaming the neighborhood, trying to spot Cy and her friends, did it occur to her: what if this whole amnesia nightmare/adventure were one big haunted house? Was her old life so full of woes and stresses that she'd just decided to leave it behind? Was *that*, deep down, the reason she couldn't remember her past? She could see the appeal: what person wouldn't be tempted by an escape into a life free of baggage and tiring memories, a life seasoned with mystery and intrigue?

Perhaps that was why she had been so quick to accept the end of her friendship with the Grogans—not just because she feared it would end soon anyway, as it had with Candy, but because she felt guilty for taking advantage of their kindness as she ran from whatever problems had chased her here. As she ran from herself.

Then again, *was* she taking advantage? The more she thought about it, the more she didn't think so. Benno was right; there was no reason her living arrangement, let alone her friendships, should end like this, and certainly not for any misperceived wrongdoing on her part. Somehow she was going to make it right with Cy and Jen. As soon as she found them.

Violet felt a little out of place without a costume, but no one seemed to take issue with her. All the families and groups of friends she saw were content to gawk at decorations, delight in the treats they'd collected, and seek out the next house with a lit-up porch light. Each time they knocked, the door would open wide and someone would appear, happy to see them whether they knew them or not. Marcy was right; Halloween did have a warmth that was all-welcoming.

A vehicle burst into view, turning from a side street. At first Violet was alarmed, given the number of pedestrians in the road. Then she saw that it was not a car but a golf cart. As it whizzed past her, she recognized Chuck Benz in the driver seat. He had two passengers, a man and a woman. They pulled over beside a gap in the line of houses, wherein stood a small playground built out of wood. Chuck twisted in his seat.

"And here on our left is the—well, your right, my left—is the Nickel Street playground, built in 1978." He stepped off the golf cart and gestured for his customers to do the same. The man was somewhat elderly and carried a walking cane; he had difficulty getting off the cart, but the woman didn't move to help him. "It was first built to serve as a recess location for the old elementary school—see that trail back there? That's how the kids came here each day. But then, a decade later, the town made the elementary school into part of the middle and high school facilities up the street there, and the old school building got converted into a mini-mall—"

"You said this was a ghost tour, not a history tour," complained the woman.

The man waved his cane irritably. "He's getting there!" he barked.

"Uh, right," Chuck stammered. "So, in the years since, the playground has been in use by just local families. And parents noticed, now and then, that some of their kids were talking to people who weren't there. But they weren't, like, saying hello; they were responding, answering questions only they could hear. When the parents asked them who they were talking to, the kids would always say, 'A lady with a funny face.'"

Violet, who had been more interested in the history than in a ghost story, started to walk on by.

"Some of the older folks who knew that, before the playground got built, this spot had been a dirty, vacant lot for as long as they could remember, started to wonder why it had been left vacant for so long. Why hadn't anybody built something on it sooner?"

Violet halted.

And then she wondered why she'd halted.

"The reason is…in the early twentieth century, the house that once stood here burned down."

She felt her heart pounding, adrenaline coursing through her veins. What was happening? Why was she suddenly on high alert?

"Some say it was a house of ill-repute, though whether that's true hasn't been confirmed. But what *is* certain is that when it burned—when someone deliberately set it on fire—at least one woman who lived there didn't make it out."

Violet tried to concentrate, endeavoring to replay in her head the moments before this instinct kicked in.

"So when the kids say their imaginary friend has a funny face…"

Stop!

There! That was it! Very faintly, Violet remembered, she'd heard a voice…

Stop!

No, not *a* voice, *Jen's* voice!

"Stop right there!"

The memory was so clear that it sounded closer—no, wait, that wasn't a memory! And it *was* closer. It came from—

Violet whirled to face the playground just in time to see someone burst through the gap in the bushes—the trail Chuck had indicated. He was dressed in overalls, wearing a metal hood with a narrow glass visor.

"Hey, cool!" Chuck exclaimed, distracted. "Someone's dressed up as Johnson's Welder!"

The Welder sprinted around the playground. A moment later, Jen tore through the bushes, tripped, went into a roll, and came up on her feet with her hand on her sidearm. Pointing at the fleeing man, she shouted, *"I said, stop!!"*

* * *

Heat blasted through the room from the tiny blue cone of flame.

Each time the sheriff or Deputy Derrick tried to approach the intruder, he directed the torch in their direction. If one of them tackled him, he could drop the torch and set the whole house on fire.

52

"What do you want?!" the sheriff hollered above the noise of the torch. "Why are you terrorizing these people?!"

The intruder gave no response but advanced on him, directing the flame his way. Derrick poised himself to rush the attacker.

"Derrick, stay right where you are! That's an order!" The sheriff backed away from the flame, colliding with the wall.

Jen, shielding Althea, could barely see, the blue flame providing the only illumination. Quickly she tapped Althea on the shoulder and signed several letters, hoping the old woman could make them out. Althea seized Jen's wrist and tugged her into the kitchen.

The sheriff felt himself sweating as the intruder closed in, the rippling flames emanating such intense heat. Vainly he tried to flatten himself against the wall. Whether the intruder intended to harm him or simply intimidate him, he wasn't sure...and in the end, he never found out.

A groan sounded from the floor nearby. The Welder slowly turned his head to regard the old woman's prone form.

Jen could hear Althea rummaging along the kitchen wall, knocking things over. Finally she gave a cry of triumph, and Jen felt a cylindrical object pressed into her hand.

"What are you doing?!" thundered the sheriff, relieved that the heat was subsiding but alarmed to see the Welder advancing toward the barely conscious woman. "You leave her alone!!"

The Welder looked up at him and tilted his head, as if to say, *Or what?*

"I swear to you, if you harm that helpless woman, I will take you down, no matter what the cost!!"

That was the moment Jen darted into the room, fire extinguisher primed and ready. She aimed and sent a jet of carbon dioxide straight at the intruder, who let out a cry.

With things happening so fast, it was only later that Jen realized how important that cry was. Between Myrna and Amy, and how frightened they'd been, Jen had begun, on some level, to believe the legend of the Welder's ghost returning to bring about more harm and terror. Now, having heard that cry, that telltale sign of vulnerability, Jen was furious at herself for giving in even a little to superstition.

She directed that fury at the intruder.

She was the first and only one to intercept him; the others stumbled and crashed about now that the only light had gone. The intruder writhed and swung his elbows at her gut; she seized one of his arms and tried to put him in an arm lock. They grappled for a moment, then he wrenched out of her grip, pushed off her and away. She heard no *bump!* signifying his running into a wall, which could only mean one thing.

She dashed in the same direction and blinked as she found herself outside, having run straight through the open front door.

Sprinting between two houses across the street was a long-legged man in overalls. Jen shot after him.

Many properties in Veil had fences along their borders, but not all. In the back of her mind, as she pursued him, Jen noted that her quarry must be familiar enough with the town to know which backyards and alleys to cut through—otherwise he'd have run himself into a dead end by now.

The man led Jen through a patch of thick bushes and trees. He tried to bend a branch to snap back at her and knock her off her feet, but she ducked just in time. "Stop!!" she hollered. Between the plant lite and the dark, she'd lost track of where she was exactly, but she was hot on his tail and intended to stay on it till she caught him. "Stop right there!!"

All of a sudden, she found herself clear of the bushes. Before her was the Nickel Street playground, and the man posing as the Welder was—already on the other side?! How had he done that?!

"I said, stop!!" Jen shouted, knowing even as she placed her hand on her sidearm that she couldn't open fire, not with all these civilians about. There were even a few standing just by the playground; they stared at her as she raced past the structure and leapt over a fire hydrant—

—and fell on her face. Evidently she hadn't jumped high enough. Her shin throbbed.

She looked up and saw the Welder haring away down the street. "No!!" She pushed herself to her feet despite the pain. Chasing him was going to hurt like hell, but she didn't care, she had to—

"Get in!"

Jen did a double take. Out of nowhere, a golf cart had pulled up beside her—with Violet in the driver seat. "Come on!" she insisted.

Jen climbed on and Violet floored it, speeding off and away even as someone behind them yelled, "Wait, stop! I have to return that!"

Violet veered between trick-or-treaters, but she kept her eyes as best she could on the man Jen was chasing. Gradually she closed the distance between them.

"Where the hell did you come from?" Jen demanded.

Violet swerved to avoid a crowd of Hobbits. "I was looking for Cy."

It would seem incredible that Jen could give Violet a suspicious look while still keeping her focus on the object of her pursuit, but somehow she managed it. "Why?"

Violet gave her an incredulous glance. "Why do you *think?!*" She looked forward again just in time to see the fugitive hop onto the curb and cut across someone's lawn. Jerking the wheel, she turned sharply into a driveway, knowing the golf cart wouldn't be able to jump the curb. She drove across the lawn and braced herself for when the cart thudded back down to the paved road.

"How much of my email did you read?!" hissed Jen.

For the first time, Violet took her eye completely off the man they were chasing. "I don't care about your email!! I just want to make up with my fr—"

Jen pointed past her. "TURN!" The fugitive had veered down another road, and Violet had shot right past him. Violet made a hard right. "No, left!" Jen shouted. "He went *left!*" But Violet continued spiraling clockwise until the golf cart had spun two hundred seventy degrees, then she floored it forward.

"What are you going to tell Cy?" Jen demanded.

"I don't want to tell her anything, I just want to work things out!" Violet yelled without looking away from the fugitive. "She's the best friend I have!"

"Work things out how? By telling her what you read?"

"I'm not trying to get between you two! What did I do to lose your trust?!"

A pickup truck made a turn just in front of the fugitive. It moved slowly, probably to keep watch for unwary trick-or-treaters. The fugitive heaved himself onto the back and hitched a ride.

"No!" Jen looked half-tempted to push Violet out and drive the cart herself. "Can't you go faster?"

"I'm trying!" The gas pedal was all the way to the floor. She stayed on the truck, but it seemed to be slowly gaining distance.

VI

Jen put her mouth close to Violet's ear. *"I decide what Cy needs to know and what she doesn't. If you understand that, then I might let you st—"* A bump in the road cut her off.

Violet shook her head firmly. "If you want me gone, you want me gone. All I want to know is why you don't believe me." She perked up as the truck slowed for another turn.

"Look," Jen said as they closed in, "I'm not saying I won't help you anymore—"

"Tell me why!!"

The truck made its turn. Violet veered to follow it, getting nearer and nearer.

"I mean it, Jen, why—"

BAM.

Both women looked up to see that the Welder had jumped off the truck *and onto the front of the golf cart.*

Violet shrieked and threw her arms across her face as he kicked at her head. Jen threw a jab straight at his groin, but he twisted and she only struck his hip.

As they fought, the golf cart, unsteered and ungassed, began to decelerate—except that just here, the street angled downward. Drawn by gravity, the cart picked up speed.

Violet managed to grab the assailant's lower leg and held on tight as he thrashed. With three of his limbs immobilized (using one leg to stand and one hand to hold on for dear life), he was unable to put up much of a defense against Jen's onslaught. Relentlessly, she pummeled whatever parts of him she could reach.

Faster and faster the golf cart zipped down the hill, much quicker than it was ever designed to travel.

Violet felt the man straining to retract his leg and tugged even harder, leaning out the side as she did so, her eyes squeezed shut.

When she opened them and saw what lay ahead, she gasped and cried out, "Jen!"

The Welder leaned down and threw a punch—not at Jen, but at Violet. He caught her in the shoulder and sent her spinning. With a yelp, she let go of the man's leg and threw out her hands, skinning them as she fell, rolling to a stop.

His limbs thus freed, the Welder dove at Jen and renewed his attack, driving punch after punch at her head and torso. But Jen answered him in kind, calling upon her training and targeting his joints, knowing she could immobilize him if he kept giving her opportunities. When next he tried to back-hand her across the face, she caught his wrist and was about to put him in an arm lock—

Violet stood up in time to see the golf cart, just reaching a row of orange cones at the bottom of the hill, suddenly soar across empty space, then pitch headlong into a deep trench.

"Jen!!!"

VII

"Your friends are looking for you."

Cy, standing by the swimming pool behind the home of her host, turned to find him approaching her. She gave him a wan smile. "I guess I've been brooding longer than I meant to."

He came to stand beside her, a foot of space between them. For a minute, they stared at the starry sky reflected in the water. A guest house stood on the far side.

After a moment, he said, "I hope there hasn't been any retaliation."

Cy looked at him. "Excuse me?"

"From that heckler a couple weeks ago, in the square. The one you defended me against."

"Oh! No. I mean…" She cleared her throat. "No, he's gone. My m-mom…made him leave town."

"Mm."

Conflicted, Cy blew a frustrated breath out through her nose. Nearby she noticed some smooth, round rocks stacked decoratively. She seized the top one and chucked it into the pool. *Shathunk!* A few deep breaths later, she murmured, "Sorry if that wasn't okay to do."

Pressler made a dismissive gesture. "I never use this pool anyway." He circled her, picked up another stone, and hurled it, making an even bigger splash. "You're right," he said. "That is cathartic."

For a moment they watched the ripples in the water, the dizzy jiggling of the moon.

"She didn't need to, you know," said Pressler, dusting off his hands. "Your mother. She didn't need to make that pest go away. You could've handled him yourself."

Cy gave it some thought and said, "Yeah. I could have." Her voice contained an odd mix of bitterness and satisfaction.

After another quick sigh, she turned about and said, "All right. Brooding time over."

"Good. Because we need one more to make up even teams for Pass the Eyeball."

"'Pass the Eyeball!?'"

"Well, it's really Pass the Orange, but—"

"Oh." Cy headed for the nearest door, reached out for the doorknob—and suddenly found her hand gripped by Pressler.

"Not that door," he said, hastily letting go of her and gesturing toward the sliding door she'd come through earlier.

She gave him a quizzical glance as he escorted her along the side of the house. "Is that the room where you keep all your deep, dark secrets?"

"Nope, just the expensive ones." He slid the door open and she stepped back into the party.

* * *

Deputy Benno's shoes thudded on the wooden planks of the footbridge over the Greene River. He played his flashlight from side to side as he strode across.

He had been on his way to Tuck Fleagle's apartment when

whom should he run into but the sheriff. Dubowski called to him as he pulled over in his patrol car, asked him what he was doing. Jen Grogan's words came back to him about investigating the wrong missing person, so Benno said, "I got a lead on Matt Foley that places him at the…" He fell silent at the scream of sirens, saw an ambulance fly down a cross-street. "Sheriff, what's happening? Do you need my help?"

Dubowski considered a moment, then said, "No. I think I've figured out what's going on. It'll be wrapped up soon. If you're close to solving Foley's disappearance, that'll be two wins in one night."

And so Benno was left feeling like he should put *some* effort into locating Foley before he pursued the Mulroy investigation further.

Benno walked the length of the bridge and came up empty. He considered examining the underside of the bridge, but that was not something he was eager to do in the dark. It would be more practical, he thought, to come back in the morning—not that there was much greater chance of finding anything important in the daytime, but still. He let the flashlight swing loose at his side as he tromped back, wondering again if it was too late at night to ask Fleagle's landlord to open—

A dark shape scuttled into view at the far end of the bridge. Benno aimed his flashlight. If it was a skunk, he wouldn't mind taking the long way round back to town. But the light revealed only a rabbit—and something else which caught his eye: what seemed to be a long, thick pole stuck into the metalwork of the bridge, just at the end. The metal frame shielded it on three sides; that's why he hadn't seen it when he first came by. Now he approached to take a closer look at it.

* * *

Delphine and Althea were going to be okay, though an ambulance had taken them to the hospital just to look them over. The paramedics from another ambulance tended to Jen and Violet's minor cuts and bruises. The only injury that still pained Jen was the one to her leg, from where she'd tripped over the fire hydrant.

That and the fact that the fugitive had gotten away. He was free, out there, possibly planning his next act of terror. Sheriff Dubowski had said he'd spotted the pattern—that the "Welder" was targeting people living on properties owned by Kurt Riner (including Delphine and Althea). The sheriff, Derrick, and a few other deputies were headed to the last inhabited property, lived in by the Hennesseys. Perhaps this time they'd catch the perp.

Jen had been ordered home due to her injury. Tonight's case had been a thrilling distraction, but she couldn't run anymore, not after fugitives and not away from her personal problems. Speaking of which…

"Violet," she said to the young woman sitting on the curb as the ambulance drove off, "I just wanted to apologize. It was unprofessional of me…" She pursed her lips. "It was downright crappy of me to harangue you while you were trying to help me."

Violet regarded her blandly. "Does that mean you've changed your mind about kicking me out?"

"No. Sorry."

Violet looked away, then shrugged. "I get it. To you I'm still a stranger—doubly so, since neither of us knows who I really am."

She seemed to be taking it incredibly well. *So why do I feel so awful about this?*

Aloud Jen said, "You should know I don't like making you leave. And I know it might not seem fair, but—"

"Fairness has nothing to do with it. Not when it comes to making decisions about your child's safety."

"R-right," said Jen, annoyed and a little unnerved that Violet had seemed to read her thoughts.

Violet stood and faced her. Though Jen towered over her, at this moment Violet seemed somehow taller. "I just want to say one thing. Whatever it is you're hiding from Cy, you should just tell her. She's going to find out sooner or later. You should know that better than I."

Jen's jaw tightened. "I know my own daughter plenty well, thank you."

"No."

"What did you say?" Jen's voice was a deadly whisper.

"I said no...I'm the one who should be thanking you. You gave me a place to stay when I had nothing. So, thank you."

Jen was at a loss. Before she could respond, Violet turned and started to walk away. "Where are you going?" Jen asked.

"Same as before. To talk to Cy."

Jen made an involuntary movement. Violet paused, as if waiting to see if Jen would try to stop her. Faltering, Jen said, "I thought you didn't know where she was."

Violet half-smiled. "We both know where she is, Jen." With that, she trotted off, not looking back.

* * *

"Allll right, everyone! You're all lovely, it's been a pleasure having you here, but it's that time." Boos—the disapproving kind—greeted Pressler's pronouncement. "Yes, I know. Just remember, you don't have to go home, but"—several guests joined in—"you can't stay here!"

"Where's Neesha?" Cy asked Em as partygoers moved en masse toward the front door.

Swiping several goodies and wrapping them in a napkin to take home, they replied, "Last I saw, she was with those people upstairs, dropping pumpkins out the window." But when they questioned the pumpkin droppers, they were told that Neesha had lost an earring out the window and had gone outside to look for it. Cy and Em proceeded to the back deck, where they called out Neesha's name.

Neesha heard them, but the gag in her mouth prevented her from responding.

Cy and Em were still calling for her when the last of the crowd filed out through the front door, and Pressler shut and locked it.

* * *

At the Spooktacular, Pressler had been inviting people left and right to his party, so Violet had heard and remembered his address. She was approaching his house when the music and the sound effects suddenly shut off, and from inside she heard a chorus of voices: "But you can't stay here!"

As a crowd of people poured out the front door, Violet stepped behind a tree, watching for Cy. She remembered the last time she'd encountered Elijah Pressler; something about him had unsettled her, so she stayed hidden as she waited.

Most of the departing guests flocked to the throng of vehicles massed along the street outside the house. Others who had come on foot began walking home. Having been in Veil more than two weeks now, Violet was beginning to recognize a great many people who lived here, by face if not by name. There was the mail carrier with the Canadian accent. There was one of the cashiers at the grocery store. There was—

Violet frowned. The man she'd just spotted—the one in his thirties with close-cropped hair, just now strolling across the front lawn—she knew him, recognized him…but she also knew she'd never seen his face before. How was that possible?

He passed crossways through the sea of guests, glancing once or twice at Pressler's house. He didn't appear to be in costume; all he had on were overalls—

Violet gasped. She *had* seen him before. It was the man Jen had been chasing! He'd been wearing a welder's mask and an acetylene tank, but she remembered his clothes, his build, the way he moved. He wasn't hiding; he was still up to no good.

The front door shut. All the guests were out. Violet scanned quickly for Cy, hoping she could convince her to call her mother or the sheriff, hoping they'd get here in time…but Cy was nowhere to be seen. Had Violet been wrong? She was so sure Cy would come here; it was exactly what any resentful teenager would do.

The man was almost out of sight. Violet darted out from behind the tree and followed him. She considered asking one of the other party-goers to call the sheriff, but something told her the most important thing was to keep track of the man, see what he was up to. Without hurrying or making it obvious, she stayed on his tail.

A little way down the road, a marker stood at the entrance to a trail through the woods surrounding these properties, denoting the path as one that led to a lookout point. The man glanced back, and Violet made a show of pretending to unlock the parked car she happened to be passing.

"Hey!"

Violet whipped around to see a middle-aged man bearing down on her. "What are you doing? That's my car!"

"Oh, sorry! Thought it was mine." Hurrying away, Violet looked back toward the man in overalls—but he'd disappeared.

* * *

As Jen trudged back toward her patrol car, her thoughts ran in circles, and it made her dizzy. She still had no idea how she and Cy were going to move forward when Cy was convinced Jen was hiding something regarding her father's death. On top of that, Cy had disobeyed her and gone to Pressler's party—not that she knew that for certain, but in her heart she knew Violet was right.

It irked her to no end that Violet—not just today, but seemingly from the moment she'd appeared—had so quickly developed a close bond with her daughter, to the point where she seemed to know her as well as an old friend or relation. Jen knew it was partly due to her own actions that she, herself, didn't share as close a bond with Cy as she used to, but she also knew she'd had no choice. She couldn't tell Cy why she'd really uprooted the two of them and brought them to Veil. As miserable as Cy had been, the alternative would've been much worse...

Wouldn't it?

Many times she'd had to remind herself—or perhaps reassure herself—that this was the right course of action. It would be so easy to lift her own burden by telling Cy the truth. It didn't feel right, lying to her. What if what she was doing was wrong? She'd tell Cy the truth eventually, of course (so Jen had told herself repeatedly). She'd tell her when Cy was ready...but would she know when that was?

Perhaps Violet would know.

The thought popped unbidden into her head, and it made Jen angry and uncomfortable. Who was this stranger who presumed to know her daughter? What did she know about what was right for her? Cy was *Jen's* daughter, and only Jen could decide what was best. She would do anything to protect Cy, even if it meant showing up at the party and dragging Cy out—

Jen stopped in her tracks.

Pressler's party.

Under the circumstances...

Pressler had asked to have his house guarded.

No, not his *house*—if that was what needed protecting, he'd have canceled the party. But something *inside* his house...

Frantically Jen pulled out her cell phone and dialed. It went straight to voicemail. Of course, on a stakeout the sheriff would've turned his phone off. Which deputy would still have a phone on? Hurriedly she dialed again.

"Hello, who is this?"

"Derrick, is the sheriff with you?"

"Grogan?"

"Derrick, quick, get the sheriff!"

"Grogan, the sheriff's busy. He's waiting, trying to catch the suspect you lost."

"It's a diversion!"

"What?"

"There's a robbery going down at Pressler's! Any minute now, dispatch is going to call Dubowski, and he'll have to choose between Pressler and—"

"Wait a minute, how do you know about a robbery?"

"Derrick, think! The sheriff's being forced into circumstances where the only way to respond to a call from Pressler is to break his commitment to Riner!"

"Pressler was just trying to make fun of our department—"

"Exactly! So when there really *is* a robbery, and the sheriff's trying to stop the person targeting Riner, he can't help Pressler without it looking like he's turning his back on Riner and caving to Pressler's whims!"

"Look, if you really think the sheriff needs to know, just call dispatch and—"

"I can't! I have a hunch the thieves are monitoring dispatch!"

"So this is all based on a hunch. That's what I thought." The line went dead.

Jen was on her own.

VIII

"Neesha!"

Cy and Em had covered most of the house, having gone back inside to search once they'd given up looking outside. The house seemed even bigger when deserted.

"Maybe Pressler would know where else we can look," Cy suggested.

But strangely they couldn't find Pressler either. They were alone in his house.

"Okay," said Em, unnerved, "I'm ready for that part of the movie where the clock chimes midnight, Halloween's over, and the scary stuff is magically gone."

"What movie's that?"

"I don't know, I could be making it up."

They had just passed the second-story window from where the pumpkins had been dropped when Cy doubled back. Looking at the ground, she saw a parallelogram of light shining on the concrete through an open door. A door that had not been open a minute ago. "There!" she cried, leading Em down the stairs and out the back. As they approached the door, Cy realized it was the one that Pressler had stopped her from—

"Hold it!"

Cy and Em jumped to see a short-haired man in overalls striding quickly toward them. Up close, they could see he was powerfully built. "Mr. Pressler's party is over," he said shortly. "You two have to leave."

"Our friend is missing," said Cy.

"Who are you?" asked Em.

"I work for Mr. Pressler," said the man. "I'm sorry, but you'll have to leave now. I'll find your friend and send her out after you."

"But we've looked all over," Cy protested. "Please, we're really worried. Do you know where Mr. Pressler is? We could ask him if there's any other place she might—"

"Mr. Pressler has gone to bed." The man took another step toward them, his face anything but friendly. "Don't make me ask you again."

"Gone to bed?" Cy and Em exchanged glances. "He hasn't gone to bed. We just looked in his bedroom."

The man's eyes narrowed.

"You know," said Em, "maybe Neesha left the party and we just didn't notice."

"Yeah," Cy nodded, "maybe you're right. We'll just—"

"Hold it right there." The man had drawn and snapped open a nasty-looking switchblade that gleamed in the moonlight. "Inside. Now." He gestured with his head toward the open door. Cy heard Em draw a frightened gasp. She put a protective arm around their shoulders as the two of them obeyed the threat.

Cy, herself, gasped the moment she entered the room. "Neesh—"

"Shut up!" The man in overalls slammed the door and shoved them against the wall. "You make one sound…" He wagged the knife in front of their eyes suggestively.

70

Cy's eyes were on Neesha, lying on the floor in what appeared to be Pressler's study, with duct tape over her mouth and binding her hands behind her. Beyond her were two men in black clothing, kneeling before a large safe. They had an array of tools surrounding them. One of them, a small, fidgety man with a widow's peak, looked back and hissed, "Are you kidding me? Two more?!"

"You finish what you're doing," ordered the man in overalls as he turned Cy and Em roughly toward the wall. "What's the sheriff up to?"

The third man, unshaven and overweight, was listening to a pair of headphones as he assisted the safecracker. "He's still at the Hennesseys', far as I can make out," he reported. "Sounds like he took the bait."

Cy felt her hands being taped together behind her, then a strip pressed over her mouth. Some muffled protests beside her told her the same had been done to Em.

"What about Pressler?" asked the man in overalls.

"Don't know."

The leader turned toward him sharply. "You're supposed to be watching the security monitor."

"Hey, come on, man! You've got me doing four jobs here— help him, listen to this, watch that, watch her." He nodded at Neesha. "Now I figure you want me to watch them, too!"

Cy and Em were yanked forward, then thrust roughly to the floor in front of a large desk with a space underneath the middle. Neesha was shoved next to them.

The man in overalls approached a large LED screen divided into multiple rectangular mini-screens, each displaying a different part of the house's interior. No movement showed on any of them, except the one showing the six of them in the office.

The man grunted. "He must be in a bathroom. He'll show up eventually. How much longer till that thing's open?"

"Ten minutes," answered the safecracker.

"Perfect."

The safecracker snorted. "Perfect would've been forcing Pressler to open this damn thing for us, or at least taking him hostage. As soon as we open the safe and his personal alarm goes off, he's gonna call in the cavalry—"

"I told you, they won't come," snapped the man in overalls. "The sheriff's loyal to Riner, Pressler's enemy. They're best buddies. It's just like our client said. He won't leave Riner to help Pressler. Soon as the safe's open, we're home free."

"What if Pressler sees us as we're making an exit?"

"What's he gonna do?"

"Well, what about them? They could identify us."

The leader turned to regard the three teenagers. "Let 'em. We know how to change appearances. Besides, it's Halloween. We're just a couple of ghosts."

The moment the men looked in her direction, Cy stopped moving. Once they looked away again, she recommenced her attempts to peel off and wriggle free of the duct tape—without making any noise. The trouble was, no matter how she twisted and bent, her fingers couldn't quite reach the—

All of a sudden, she felt another pair of hands working at the duct tape, stripping it away as quietly as possible. Cy looked over, but Em and Neesha were still bound. She started to turn farther to see behind her.

"Don't look!" whispered a tiny voice.

Cy's eyes went wide.

The leader glanced her way again, and she blinked rapidly, hiding her surprise as best she could, all the while wondering—

How did Violet get here???

* * *

Though she hadn't seen the man in overalls take it, the lookout trail seemed the most logical choice. Violet followed it, thankful the moon provided some illumination. It wasn't long before she came to a spot where the trail split. The second trail branched off to the right, with a sign stuck dead center: PRIVATE PROPERTY. *Pressler's,* she thought. This other trail must lead to his house.

Perhaps she ought to have weighed her options before going on, but in thinking about it, she reasoned, she probably would've reached the same decision anyway.

A minute later she spied the back of Pressler's mansion, flanked by a swimming pool and a small guest house. One door was open; there were lights on inside. She glimpsed people moving about. She tiptoed over—and was shocked to see Cy's friend Neesha trussed up within. Three men surrounded her, one of them the fugitive in overalls, the others trying to break into a safe.

"Neesha!" Cy's voice issued from a window upstairs. The fugitive dashed from the house.

His cohorts weren't watching the door. Instinct took over: Violet darted across the open space, through the door and behind a desk. Hopefully she'd soon have an opportunity to rescue Neesha.

Her heart sank when Cy and Em were captured as well, but when all three teens were set against the desk, it put their bound hands in an ideal position for Violet. She crawled silently beneath the desk and began stripping the duct tape from Cy's wrists. "Don't look!" she hissed when Cy started to turn. A minute later she moved on to Neesha.

"How much longer?" demanded the man in overalls, clearly the leader of the thieves.

"Almost there," replied the safecracker.

Violet could say the same. Neesha and Cy were freed of their bonds (though they kept their hands hidden from their captors), and she was just about finished with Em—

"Hello??"

Everyone looked up. Violet remembered just in time not to bang her head on the underside of the desk and give herself away.

"Anyone here? Mr. Pressler?" The voice was coming from the front of the house.

"Who is that?" the safecracker hissed.

Darkly the leader whispered, "I know who that is."

"I'm Deputy Grogan from the sheriff's department. Is everything all right here?"

Cy made a noise through the tape covering her mouth, prompting an order from the leader to be silent. To his accomplices he said, "I'll deal with this. Get the bonds and meet me at the van." With that he unlocked the inner door and slipped out.

Jen's voice came again, in a measured, casual tone: "Looks like the party was a success. I'm glad I'm not on clean-up duty here." Had anyone been watching the monitors, they'd have seen her peering carefully through a doorway into the next room.

With Em finally freed, Violet cautiously poked her head up from behind the desk. The two remaining thieves were too absorbed in their task to notice their hostages. Violet slunk to the outer door and motioned to Cy and the others. Slowly, fearful the slightest motion might attract the thieves' attention, the three teens crawled toward Violet.

On the monitor, Jen padded toward the next door, keeping close to the wall. Unbeknownst to her, the lead thief lurked above her on the second-floor balcony. He toted something heavy.

The teens were on their feet now. Violet twisted the doorknob, began to ease the door open...

"Got it!" The safecracker's exclamation made the kids jump, but the thieves were distracted by the now-open safe and what it contained.

The man in overalls raised the object over the balcony railing, directly above Jen's head.

Glancing at the monitor, Cy saw him—about to drop a heavy doorstop—

She ripped the duct tape off her mouth. *"MOM!!!"*

The thieves looked up.

Jen doubled back. "Cy?!"

The doorstop dropped and dented the floor beside Jen's feet. She jumped, looked up in time to see a figure flitting away.

The overweight man lunged at Cy. Violet threw her entire body weight into him—which wasn't much, but fortunately her shoulder caught him in the solar plexus. Then she shoved Cy out with the others and slammed the door behind them. When the man caught Violet by the shoulders, she kicked and swung at him wildly, though nothing landed. He threw her aside, but she dove straight back at him, raking at his face and his hair.

The safecracker reached into the safe, grabbed a stack of bonds, and made for the inner door. At the last moment, hearing footsteps, he darted to the side. When the door swung open, he was hidden behind it.

Violet doubled over as the man drove his fist into her stomach. Next moment, from out of nowhere a flurry of blows landed him senseless on the floor. "Where's Cy?" Jen demanded. Violet pointed at the outer door, unable to speak. Jen reached for the doorknob but found that, in the course of the fight, the doorknob had been broken off.

Cy, Em, and Neesha sprinted around the side of the house—and then abruptly skidded to a halt. The thieves' leader rose from the shadows like a specter, forcing them to double back, tripping over themselves. None of them knew about the path from the back of the property to the lookout trail, or else they would've chosen that avenue of escape. As it was, Cy hauled open the sliding glass door, then tugged it shut once they were all inside again, just as the man approached. Cy quickly locked the door but then fled when the man snatched up a rock. She heard the glass shatter as she scrambled up the back stairs with the others.

Briskly the safecracker made his way toward the front of the house. He was just passing a closet when WHAM! The closet door burst open, knocking him clean off his feet. He was out cold before he hit the floor.

Pressler spared him a cursory glance before he made off in haste.

Seconds later, Jen and Violet came across the downed intruder. Jen passed him by, calling again for her daughter. Violet paused just long enough to curiously pick up the dropped bonds.

Neesha, Em, and Cy tore through the second floor and down the front staircase. With a glance back, it looked to Cy like they'd lost their pursuer.

As Neesha pawed frantically at the front door, Jen and Violet entered from another room. For a moment, Cy felt relief, which quickly turned to fright as the man in overalls appeared above them. She cried out a warning, but rather than drop another heavy object over the side, he ran straight at the balcony, vaulted over it, landed on the ground floor, and went immediately into a roll.

Cy read his intentions in the nick of time. As he came up from the roll she threw her arms out, shoving Em back. Thus, it was Cy the man caught from behind, putting the tip of his knife to her throat.

"Let her go!" Jen ordered, her weapon drawn, safety off.

"Drop it!" the man shot back. "Drop it right now! I know this is your kid!" He squeezed Cy tighter to him. Her eyes were shut tight, her lips drawn back.

Muttering a prayer, Jen put the safety back on. As she lowered the weapon to the floor, Violet rushed forward and held out the sheaf of bonds. "Here!" she pleaded. "Here, take them! They're what you wanted, aren't they? Just take them and let her go!"

The man touched his lips to Cy's ear. "You move, I open your throat." Keeping the knife to her neck, he reached out and took the bonds, stuffing them down his collar.

"Now let her go," Jen growled.

"I don't think so." The man dragged Cy to the front door, reached back, and pulled it open.

"Holy—!" Neesha took a step back. Everyone else gasped.

The thief spun around.

Standing in the doorway was Johnson's Welder.

Overalls. A metal facemask. An acetylene tank worn on the back, flaming torch in hand. Everything older and dirtier than what the false Welder had donned for his costume.

Cy heard the thief draw a frightened breath.

Instantly he threw Cy toward the specter and doubled straight back—whereupon his face met Jen's fist. Several times.

The Welder, having deactivated the torch, helped steady Cy on her feet, but then wobbled on his own. One of his legs had a limp.

Jen caught Cy's arm and pulled her into a tight embrace. Then, as everyone caught their breath, she squinted at the Welder. "Myrna? Is that you?"

The Welder tipped up the visor. "Of course it's me," said Myrna. "You called and said you needed backup, remember?" She pointed at Cy. "'S this your kid? She's cute."

Jen pinched the bridge of her nose. "Myrna, I asked you to keep *calling* for backup. To keep trying to reach the sheriff. And what are you…? Why are you…?"

Myrna glanced down at her getup, then at the fallen, would-be thief, and shrugged. "Why not?"

IX

"The bathroom," the sheriff repeated skeptically.

"That's right," said Pressler. "I'd been, ahem, holding it the last twenty minutes of the party. Didn't wanna be rude. Once everyone was gone—or so I thought—I went in there, and I was still…occupied when all the ruckus started. I couldn't have come out even if I'd wanted to."

The sheriff leaned forward and interlaced his fingers on his desk. "Those bonds in your safe—that's the reason you asked for some deputies to be on guard at your house tonight."

"Yes. The bonds weren't supposed to arrive till tomorrow. I'd planned to take them straight to the bank. By mistake, they came today, and the bank was closed."

"Why didn't you just bring them to me, if they're so valuable? My department could've looked after them."

Pressler shrugged. "I thought of doing that, but after our… misunderstanding earlier today, I wasn't sure if you'd say yes."

For a minute they stared at each other in silence, one of them chipper and calm, the other wary and fatigued.

"Well, if that's all, may I go?" asked Pressler.

"One more thing. We had a word with these would-be thieves." Dubowski rose slowly to his feet. "They say they used to work for you."

"For me?" Pressler chuckled. "I doubt that."

"They say you hired them under the table—several times. That you rarely interacted with them in person. Paid them to do illegal things. They made a list. It's not short."

"Well, what do you expect them to say, Sheriff? They tried to rob me. They were caught. The best they can do is fire a parting shot."

"We found evidence they were once in possession of a *silver SUV*. Like the one that rammed Deputy Benno's patrol car two weeks ago."

Despite the baleful look Dubowski was giving him, Pressler shrugged blithely as he stood up. "I don't know what to tell you, Sheriff. Only that I'd...be more careful if I were you."

"Excuse me?"

Pressler had opened the door, but he turned back to say, "You don't want to go casting malicious aspersions—especially not after the position you put yourself in tonight. Everyone knows you brushed off my request for help from your department—a request we now know was valid. And what were you doing when I was being robbed? You were chasing a ghost. An imaginary spook—oh, but I forgot, the spook targeted your *friend*, Kurt Riner. I guess it pays to be personal friends with the sheriff. *Then* you can count on his protection."

"Jesus...!" Dubowski took an unsteady step backward. "You... you set this up. Everything—the Welder, the bonds, the party— all to discredit me and swing more voters."

In a quiet voice, Pressler replied, "Like I said, Sheriff...I'd be more careful." He closed the door on the sheriff's pale, dumbstruck face.

"You caused all this...just to get ahead in a stupid election?"

Pressler pivoted to find Violet staring at him with fiery eyes.

"You frightened all those people, injured some of them, put Cy and her friends in danger—"

"No," Pressler said sharply, taking a step toward her and pointing. "Cyanne was in no danger whatsoever—until *you* interfered." He sounded genuinely angry.

"You wanna tell that to her?" asked Violet.

Pressler's lip curled. "Neither of us is going to tell her."

Violet raised an eyebrow. "Is that a threat?"

Pressler folded his arms. "I heard you tell the sheriff you knew Cyanne had gone to my house because her mother forbade it. But you were wrong. That's not why she went. Cyanne is still grieving, vulnerable, reeling from her father's sudden departure from her life."

Violet looked at him askance. "What, and you think you're filling that hole in her life? A new father figure?"

"If I were…could you take that away from her?"

Violet felt uncertainty seeping in and tried not to let it show, but it must have, for Pressler's lips gave a smug twitch. As he sauntered toward the exit, he drawled, "Try to remember, 'Violet,'" he seemed amused by her name, "real change is brought about by real people. And real people have identities."

Her voice stopped him on the threshold. "Well, if I'm not a person…then I guess that makes me a ghost. And ghosts are known for haunting people."

Pressler scowled at her.

She waved at him. "Happy Halloween, Mr. Pressler."

He gave one last snort—which sounded only a little forced— as he departed.

"So," said a voice, making Violet jump, "are you gonna tell her?"

"What?"

"Cy," said Jen, stepping out of the darkened doorway across the hall. "Are you going to tell her about Pressler?"

"Of course I am…I think. I mean…" She trailed off, overcome with mounting ambivalence.

Then she looked at Jen and asked, "What do *you* think?"

Jen was too well-trained to let it show, but at that moment, within her there occurred a series of revelations. First, that what she had feared Violet would bring about was never really a cause for worry; that was only an excuse. In actuality, Violet made her uncomfortably aware of a conflict that had already existed. It was the conflict—*not* Violet—that was the true danger. And that conflict stemmed from something inside her…or, rather, a *lack* of something.

Now, as Violet spoke those words, deferring to Jen's judgment as if it were the natural thing to do, Jen felt as if a burden were lifted from her shoulders—no, that wasn't quite it. The burden was still there, just as heavy as before, but Jen suddenly found herself able to shoulder it, to carry it without difficulty.

It took Jen several moments to fully take it in. She was almost startled to find Violet still there, waiting for an answer.

Clearing her throat, Jen replied, "You really didn't read my email, did you."

Violet opened her mouth but didn't respond.

"No," said Jen, "of course you didn't. I'm sorry. I'm…dealing with something, and it has nothing to do with you. I shouldn't have…"

"It's okay," said Violet. "I know you didn't plan to have me staying with you this long. It probably takes roommates a while to get used to each other. I mean, not that we're going to be— anymore, but…"

"Violet, you can stay in our house as long as you want."

Violet was speechless. Her eyes closed in relief.

"Come on," said Jen, patting her on the arm. "Let's go home."

* * *

"Cyanne."

"Oh no."

They'd reached the Grogan house, stopping briefly at the square to pick up Cy's bicycle. They'd just made it into the kitchen when Jen used her daughter's full name, causing Cy to deflate. "Please, Mom, can we not do this now? I'm tired and I just want to—"

"Rob's missing."

A shivery jolt passed through Cy's body. "What did you say?"

"Rob Mulroy, your ex-boyfriend—"

"I know who Rob is!!"

"Has been missing for over two weeks. When you thanked me for running him out of town, I had no idea what you were talking about."

Mother and daughter stared at each other from opposite ends of the room. Violet watched from off to the side, just inside the back door, unsure whether she should make herself scarce.

Cy pointed. "But you said—"

"I lied. I could see you were relieved he was gone. I didn't want to make you worry he might still be around. I should've told you the truth. I'm sorry. I made a mistake. It wasn't the first and it won't be the last. I'm always trying to do better."

Cy shook her head, flabbergasted. "I—"

"But that does *not* make it okay, what you did!" Cy cringed away as Jen advanced on her. "I knew there might be danger at Pressler's party, even though I didn't know what kind. That's why I told you not to go."

"I'm sorry—"

"You disobeyed me out of spite, and you and your friends could've gotten seriously hurt—"

"Mom, I'm sorry!"

"That's not good enough!"

Cy threw up her hands helplessly. Her eyes watered. "I didn't do it—just to spite you!" she said through sniffles.

"I know," said Jen in a softer voice. "I know it's more than that. I think…you've lost faith in me." She directed a momentary glance at Violet.

"Well—!" Cy's voice rose in pitch. "How am I supposed to have faith in you when you don't—"

"Cy, I could spend a lifetime trying to prove myself, explaining my actions till I'm blue in the face, and it wouldn't fix things. Believe me, I know. I'll do my best to earn back your trust, but *the choice still has to come from you.* It won't be a choice you can make like that." She snapped her fingers. "It'll take time. All I need is for you to try."

Cy stood there, chest heaving with emotion, her eyes wavering between defiance and acquiescence. Jen waited patiently for her answer.

A sneeze made them both glance over. "Sorry," Violet whispered.

Finally Cy shrugged. "Fine. I'll try. Of course I'll try."

"Thank you."

After an awkward pause, Cy mumbled something about taking a shower and went upstairs.

"Jen?" Violet stepped toward her.

Jen turned to face her. "Violet, I never thanked you for helping earlier—with the golf cart. And later, at Pressler's house—"

"Jen," said Violet as the noise of Cy's shower issued from upstairs, "I have to tell you something."

Jen closed her eyes for a moment, inhaling through her nose. "Go ahead."

"The way my memory works… Oftentimes I see or hear something and it triggers a memory of something I didn't know I saw."

In spite of herself, Jen chuckled. "You didn't read my email, but…"

"I saw it." Violet swallowed. "And when we were at Pressler's, I saw Cy and her friends tied up with duct tape."

Jen frowned, not understanding.

"I saw them…*restrained*."

It took a moment for Jen to comprehend. When she did, she uttered a long, low groan as she sank onto the wooden bench by the table.

In a low voice, Violet said, "I'm sorry."

Jen looked up at her. "So…you know."

"Y-yeah."

"And you think I should tell Cy the truth."

Violet hesitated. "No."

Jen stared at her a moment, then rose back to her feet. "No?"

Violet shook her head decisively. "I think you were right not to tell her, for what it's worth. I don't think she should ever find out."

Epilogue

Sheriff Dubowski slouched in his chair, arms on the armrests, his face in a grimace. Grogan had warned him. Multiple times. He'd still walked straight into it.

Deputy Derrick appeared in his office doorway, saw the sheriff was in low spirits. He opened his mouth, perhaps to offer some words of reassurance.

Dubowski looked at him with only his eyes while the rest of him remained still. The effect was not encouraging.

Recognizing that he was still in the doghouse for not passing along Grogan's message, Derrick wisely moved on without speaking. Perhaps now the embittered deputy would acknowledge Grogan's value to the team. Or maybe he'd be more resentful than ever. The sheriff sighed.

Similarly, he thought, he could either learn from this failure or wallow in his own self-pity. At least he'd be more on his guard now against any further trickery from Pressler. The election was still weeks away; whatever damage he'd done to Kurt's campaign could be repaired. As long as nothing else too important came up.

Another deputy appeared in the doorway. "Benno!" the sheriff greeted him, sitting up. "How'd that lead on Foley turn out? Got any good news for me?"

Deputy Benno trod heavily into the office. He held an item in each hand, one large, one small, both in plastic evidence bags.

His face was ashen, grave.

Dubowski eyed him uncertainly. "Benno?"

Benno set the larger of the two items on the desk; it made a heavy, solid sound. Through the plastic Dubowski could see it was a thick tree branch, possibly birch. It had been whittled and smoothed to form a serviceable club or walking stick. One end was covered in red splotches. "What is this?" asked the sheriff.

Benno swallowed. "Sheriff...I think we have a serial killer in Veil." He set down the other item, the one he'd found upon searching Tuck Fleagle's apartment. It was a digital audio recorder. Benno pressed the "play" button.

"Someone's here!" gasped an old man's voice. *"Someone followed us! Followed you!"*

"No one followed me!"

The sheriff looked up. "Is that Rob Mulroy?"

"Yes, they did! They want to stop me from telling you!"

"Telling me what? Who's 'they?' Hey!"

"Let me go! They'll kill me!"

"Just tell me—"

"Let me go—"

A loud but distant *pop* seemed to cut the voices off.

* * *

"Hey, Vi?"

Violet looked over from the desk, the landline receiver in her hand.

Cy, no longer covered in fake blood, was dressed in a light blue bathrobe, her hair still damp. She looked contrite as she approached. "I just wanted to apologize. I'm sorry I accused you and dragged you into my drama."

After a short pause, Violet hung up the phone and hugged Cy. "I'm just glad you're okay," she said.

"Yeah, that's, like, the third or fourth time you and Mom have saved me. Next time we have a crisis, it's my turn to do the saving."

"It's a deal," said Violet.

As they pulled away, Cy asked, "Who were you calling?"

"You remember Marcy, that witch at the sabbat who did the smudging? She invited me to hang out tonight."

"You're going out again?"

"No, but I wanted to call her and ask for a rain check. Might as well start developing a circle of friends around here, if I can."

"Nice. Good for you. So what'd she say?"

"Well, she's not answering. I'll call her one more time, then I'll try again tomorrow." She re-dialed Marcy's number.

Lying on the ground, Marcy's phone rang. Beside it, hidden beneath a slide in the Nickel Street playground, lay Marcy herself, on her back, staring up sightlessly.

A hand reached under the slide. A black substance was sprinkled over the young woman's face, speckling her unblinking eyes.

That was how she was found the next morning.

WINTER IN VEIL

A Mystery Novella Series
by Miles Ledoux

Next time in Veil...

Jen's fingers brushed the handle of her sidearm. "To anyone who can hear me," she said in a clear, no-nonsense voice, "I'm Deputy Grogan of the Veil sheriff's department. If you belong in this house, please say something so I can help you." She paced slowly through the living room, back toward the front of the house. "If you *don't* belong here, you need to make your presence known *now.*"

She waited.

All at once, she heard a scream.

It came from upstairs. Jen tore up the steps, all the while hearing more screams, louder, more intense.

By the time she burst through the door at the top, her weapon was out.

About the Author

Miles Ledoux was born in upstate New York and started writing murder mysteries at the age of nine. His first paid writing gig was in 2007, when a local theatre chose one of his plays for their summer melodrama. He received other royalties after moving to Los Angeles for graduate school, where he wrote, directed, and produced several mystery dessert theatre plays. He also started a side business designing and running mystery party games while working as a martial arts instructor.

Currently the author resides in Springfield, Vermont. Despite having lived in five different states, he has remained active in community theatre as a playwright, director, and actor. He also has a YouTube channel where he compares Agatha Christie adaptations to the books they were based on. His handle is @MysteryMiles.

Miles loves books, cats, music, Star Trek, Peanuts, and owns an ever-growing number of variations of the board game Clue. His favorite author is Lloyd Alexander.

You can connect with me on:

🌐 https://www.ledouxmysteries.com